MARK BANNERMAN

THE EARLY LYNCHING

Complete and Unabridged

LINFORD
Leicester

First published in Great Britain in 1997 by
Robert Hale Limited, London

First Linford Edition
published 1999
by arrangement with
Robert Hale Limited, London

British Library CIP Data

Bannerman, Mark
    The early lynching.—Large print ed.—
    Linford western library
    1. Western stories
    2. Large type books
    I. Title
    823.9′14 [F]

    ISBN 0–7089–5413–8

Published by
F. A. Thorpe (Publishing) Ltd.
Anstey, Leicestershire

Set by Words & Graphics Ltd.
Anstey, Leicestershire
Printed and bound in Great Britain by
T. J. International Ltd., Padstow, Cornwall

This book is printed on acid-free paper

THE EARLY LYNCHING

Young Rice Sheridan leaves behind his adoptive Comanche parents and finds work on the Double Star Ranch. Three years later, he and his boss, Seth Early, are ambushed by outlaws, and their leader, the formidable Vince Corby, brutally murders Early. Rice survives and reaches town. Pitched into a maelstrom of deception and treachery, Rice is nevertheless determined that nothing will prevent him from taking revenge on Corby. But he faces death at every turn . . .

Books by Mark Bannerman
in the Linford Western Library:

ESCAPE TO PURGATORY

JG

F

BANNERMAN

The early lynching

LARGE PRINT   £8.50

C.95

L 5/9

For Jim

1

After eighteen-year-old Rice Sheridan was shot in the leg by Vince Corby, he was taken to the surgery at Bull Crossing. His trousers were sodden with blood and he was out of his mind with shock. Doc Finnegan curtailed his drinking spree at the local saloon and bedded Rice in the room above his drugstore. Here, the doctor's elfin-faced wife Maggie fussed over the young cowboy, her big hazel eyes full of compassion as she peeped around the black swirl of her hair. Amid his ravings, Rice wondered how on earth a sixty-year-old drunkard like Finnegan, who constantly rambled on about taking retirement, had gotten himself a wife so youthful and downright lovely, but he had little time to speculate. Finnegan dropped a tincture of laudanum on to his tongue, sent him skimming into a twilight world where pain got lost and all concerns were held in abeyance.

Amid the drifting mists of his consciousness, Rice breathed in the overwhelming smell of carbolic. He was sometimes aware of Maggie's sweet, encouraging voice and of Doc fretting over the bandages, cursing in his slurred Irishness. On the fifth day, Finnegan pulled open the curtains and allowed the Texas sun to flood the room. He'd withheld the laudanum so that Rice's awareness took stronger hold. Now the pain returned, seeping up through his thigh and into every cranny of his body. He wondered if Vince Corby would come searching for him. Hatred for the man rose in him with the bitterness of bile, had him groaning with anguish. He tensed as he heard footsteps thudding along the boardwalk beneath the window, but then he slumped back. He could also hear wagons rolling down the street outside, harness jingling, and the babble of folks' voices all the normal, every-day sounds of town life.

He felt woozy with fever, but suddenly Finnegan's face appeared in his range of vision and the Irishman's unusually sober expression jarred Rice's concentration into focus. The doctor had eased the soggy bandage away from the wound, wrinkling his nose. 'Sure don't smell so good, kid.'

'Maybe it needs a good clean cut,' Rice gasped.

Finnegan shook his white shaggy head, cursing softly. A sweetish, fetid odour had Rice's stomach turning.

'Putrid,' Finnegan said.

Rice groaned and risked a downward look, catching a glimpse of greenish yellow flesh. It was seeping pus. 'It ain't gonna kill me, is it, Doc?' His voice came as a hoarse rasp, pleading for hope.

Finnegan averted his eyes. 'I think we both need a drink, kid.'

As the doctor turned away, Rice rested down on his pillow. He'd never figured this sort of thing would happen to him — young, crazy wild Rice Sheridan, named Head-Touches-the-Clouds by the Indians who had reared him. Rice Sheridan who'd always stood rock-firm on his own two feet and handed out as much punishment as he took. Now everything was changing.

Finnegan uncorked a bottle and started to pour liquor into glasses. 'Best whiskey this side of the Missouri River,' he remarked. 'Made from raw alcohol, black chewing baccy, water from the Big Muddy . . . and rattlesnake heads. It'll rot your guts but it does wonders for pain.'

'Doc,' Rice groaned, 'give it to me straight. What are my chances? You ain't gonna cut my leg off, are you?' He could feel the trembling in him. The fever, he thought, the damned fever's turning me into a quaking leaf — but he knew it was fear too. He'd never felt so gut-scared in his life. That, coupled with the black hatred he felt for Corby, made him angry.

Finnegan had walked over to the

bedside with the filled glasses. 'Tip this back, kid, then I'll give you the low-down and . . . ' Suddenly he hesitated. 'No. Maybe you best stay off the hard stuff. With so much laudanum swilling round inside you, this would most likely finish you off. I'll have to drink them both, I guess.' He sat down alongside the bed and tried to soften his words. 'Kid . . . I been in medicine for forty-five years, figure on retiring soon. I seen a lot, done a lot, but I'm not a surgeon, never qualified, though I've done my share of holding down while surgeons do the cutting. I've got a friend over at Fort Lovell, name of Arnold Sabine. He's an army surgeon, did a lot o' good work during the war, at Shiloh and Chickamauga. That was hell on earth, to be sure.'

'I know,' Rice grunted, impatient to get to the point.

'Well, like I say, I'd sooner not do the job single-handed. I'll ask Sabine to come over and do the actual surgery. He owes me a drink or two. You can rest assured, he's the best sawbones in the business.'

'What are you sayin', Doc?'

'What I'm telling you is that unless the job is done pretty soon, you're going to die. You're burning with fever and the gangrene will spread up your leg.'

Words sliced through Rice's mind: *He's gonna ask this fella Sabine to come over from Fort Lovell . . . and cut my leg off?*

Finnegan drained the second whiskey. 'It's the only way, kid, that's if you want to stay this side of the Golden Gate.' He put his glass down on the table. 'All being well, Arnold Sabine'll be here tomorrow. You're big and strong as an ox. You'll get over it OK.'

Rice used the Comanche curse words he had learned long ago. He was trapped just as tightly as if he'd been behind iron bars.

Maggie had come quietly into the room, standing just behind her husband, her hazel eyes brimming with sympathy. A single tear was trickling down her cheek. She brushed it away with her slim hand, as if annoyed with herself for allowing her emotions to show. Rice thought, she's the nearest thing to an angel I'll ever know.

He felt his eyelids sag. Why couldn't Corby's bullet have lodged somewhere more vital, put him beyond pain and the surgeon's knife? He'd heard that after amputation, you could feel the hurt in the absent limb, just as if it was still there.

Weakness was misting his brain. Suddenly he was drifting back into the past. He'd go over everything in his head, dream his way through the whole crazy chain of events. Maybe, if he was really smart, he could change things around so he could escape the awesome mess he was now in. Maybe . . .

2

Rice's boss Seth Early had told him the story many times, always softening his voice so as to state the brutal facts as mercifully as he could. 'The Indians were Kaitsenko Kiowa under chief Sittin' Bear. They hit your folks' cabin, fired flamin' arrows into the roof. Your ma and pa never stood a chance. I guess they died as quick as they could do under such circumstances.'

Rice would nod his dark head sadly. 'How the hell I got out, God only knows.'

'Your ma must've pushed you through the back window just minutes before she died.'

Rice had been scarcely two years old on that awful day, too young to recall the nightmare events which had orphaned him, but Seth Early had always answered his questions patiently, implanting the scene as clearly in his mind as if it had come from first-hand memory.

'It was a sure-fire miracle that you escaped the flames, toddled up the path behind the cabin into the hills. Thankfully them murderous Kiowa never tracked you down, killed you the same as they did so many white kids. Lucky for you it was Quohada Comanches who found you wanderin' the desert next day. Thank God they were friendly with the whites right then.'

True enough, his survival had been nothing short of amazing. The Comanche Kicking Horse and his wife White Calf had visited his parents only a week before the massacre, had traded provisions. They took the orphaned child into their family, reared him as their own. Thus, Rice grew up on the rugged Staked Plains, west of the Pecos River. When he was four he was given a bow and blunt arrows. As he grew older he received larger, stronger bows and he was shown how to stalk small game and hit moving targets. He played with other boys, engaging in shooting matches and sham battles, showing a courage that made his adoptive parents proud. Later, he learned to ride.

When he was eight, the Quohadas signed a treaty with the whites and moved on to a reservation near Fort Sill. Here, Rice attended the agency school, learning English and the written word. He had long dark hair and swarthy, suntanned features and his appearance was similar to that of the Indian children. Only two things set him apart: he was taller than most of his stocky contemporaries and he showed an aptitude for the teachings that left the schoolmarm astounded.

But his education was cut short. The Comanche chief Quanah Parker had remained wild; now he called on all Indians to return to their old ways. Accordingly, Kicking Horse and many others, together with their families, deserted the reservation and pitched their villages deep on the inhospitable Staked Plains. Rice went with them.

From his questioning of Kicking Horse, he had learned the terrible fate of his true parents. Once, he even returned to the spot where the cabin had stood, in a valley near the head of the Fresno Canyon. Here, the long-horned, brown and white buffalo of the white man now grazed. He had seen how the elements had nigh destroyed all trace of human habitation, apart from the depression where the root cellar had been. Kneeling down, he sifted the earth through his fingers and shed tears for his white ma and pa. Hatred had grown in him for their murderers — the Kaitsenko Kiowa. He swore that when he was a man, he would seek them out and destroy them. But the seed of vengeance inside him was snuffed out. Through the Indian grapevine came the news that the Kaitsenko band had been cut down by bluecoats, and that Sitting Bear himself had fallen, his body riddled by countless bullets. Rice had grunted with satisfaction, hoping that the killers of his parents had not died too quickly.

Approaching manhood, he was given his formal Indian name — Head-Touches-the-Clouds, because he was over six feet tall. By now, he was becoming more and more aware of the increased hostility, the bitterness, between the Comanches and the whites. There had been clashes with both bluecoats and Texas Rangers, and now Quanah Parker was inciting the tribes to throw out the encroaching settlers and soldiers. To his dismay, Rice realized that the Comanches were striking at homesteaders with the same savagery as the Kiowa had shown, and a brooding uneasiness grew in him.

At this time he purified himself in a sweat lodge and undertook the vision quest that was the custom for all Indian boys after they had passed through puberty. On foot, he went alone into the hills. He was stripped down to a breech-clout and he carried no food or weapons. He walked through the night, the wind moaning between crevices in the far bluffs, sounding like the warnings of spirits. He shivered and was afraid. Long after the moon had lifted, painting the world a silver ghost-grey, he lay down on the grass and he could hear a wolf howling. Even so, he slept soundly, undisturbed by dreams.

Next morning, hunger gnawed like a rodent in his belly. He allowed his thoughts to wander, to drift over everything that had happened to him. In his mind, he saw his white parents; they were laughing and happy — then the war-cries of the Kiowa sounded, causing him to writhe in his inability to reach back across the years, to save his ma and pa. Later, he pondered on the very Comanches who had reared him, now turning on the settlers, burning their cabins, killing man, woman and child.

On the third night, still without food, he dreamed he fell from a high cliff and the wind was screaming in his ears.

He awoke, shivering in the night air. And suddenly he could hear Quanah Parker's voice, seeming to come from the sky: 'You must fight with us, Head-Touches-the-Clouds. You must help us — or go back to the whites. You cannot be an in-between man.'

The words echoed in his head, over and over: *You cannot be an in-between man*.

Again he slept, and this time he dreamed of his parents, struggling for their lives as Indians swept down from the valley-rim, and leading the Indians was a youth with a familiar face. Suddenly he realized it was his own!

'No!' He snapped awake, crying out in anguish. He leaped up, his mind whirling in dizzy circles, his heart pounding like a trip-hammer. He thought of Kicking Horse and White Calf, and of his Indian brothers and sisters. Though he loved them, he was forever aware that there was no Indian blood in his veins.

By the time he rested down again,

3

Seth Early and his younger brother Able owned the Double Star Ranch and the far-flung acres that stretched to the Pecos River. The Earlys had taken full advantage of the great boom in the cattle market. Some folks said they had more money than was decent. Even so, they'd been lacking in one important commodity since their mother had died two years back, and that was female comfort. Women were rare, even at Bull Crossing, apart from those you paid money for. Seth Early had felt the scarcity badly and figured if he didn't act quickly he'd never get the son he longed for. He'd taken to viewing the catalogues that came in from the East, particularly the personal columns where females advertised for husbands. Of course Early had plenty to offer in the way of wealth and security, and when he'd become smitten with the picture of one particular New York lady and corresponded with her, she'd been only too pleased to accept his proposal of marriage. Her name was Gabriella Devaney.

Life had seemed good on that sunny day three years after Rice had started work on the ranch, when Seth Early and he rode over Travis Mountain towards the town of Bull Crossing. They were on their way to Seth Early's wedding. Rice had had his dark hair cut short and they were togged in their Sunday-best, with boiled shirts, new worsted suits and Stetsons. Being tall, Rice found his suit a skimpy fit, despite the fact that Early had paid twelve dollars for it, but as he'd be wearing it for no more than a couple of days, he wasn't too concerned. They'd shared a bottle of whiskey and felt merry. It was early spring, blue jays were chattering, arcing saucily above their heads, chipmunks darted along the branches and the pine-scented, mountain air was good to breathe. When they rested, allowing their horses to suck noisily from a stream which cascaded over some rocks, they rolled cigarettes and lit up and Early took the torn-out page of the catalogue from his pocket, his blue eyes shining as he gazed at the picture on it.

'I guess she's the most beautiful female I ever saw,' he murmured. He looked proud, and Rice felt honoured that he'd chosen him, a humble cowpoke, to ride along and make sure the wedding arrangements went without hiccup. In fact Early had seemed to take a shine to the tall, Indian-looking boy ever since he'd started work at the Double Star.

Rice had always known that his second name was Sheridan, but he'd never learned what his given name was. Head-Touches-the-Clouds was too much of a mouthful, so one evening when he'd been given supper at the Earlys' table, Seth had jokingly dubbed him after the pudding they were eating, rice, and the name had stuck thereafter.

Seth Early was now in his forties, whip-cord slim, an upright man with a ready smile when he was pleased. He claimed he had a direct line to the Lord, and Rice had seen him praying more than once. A closeness had grown between the rancher and his young hand. Rice, wondering why this was so, later concluded that Early treated him like the son he hoped to have one day. Similarly, Rice had settled in well with the ranch foreman, Brad Silvers, the trail boss Will Carver, and the many hired hands who drifted in and out of employment. All respected his capacity for hard work.

Seth Early had always taken a personal interest in educating the quick-learning Rice in cattle-work, teaching him the skills of rounding-up beasts, herding them on the home range in readiness for the drive north. Brad Silvers had taught him the skills of the lariat, roping horses and fiery long-horned steers; he'd shown him how to brand animals with the double-star, how to castrate calves, how to 'cut' selected animals from the herd. Additionally, the long drive up the Chisholm Trail had been an education in itself.

Now, in Rice's pocket was the wad of money Early had given him to meet the inevitable wedding expenses, and he was determined to spend it wisely and not let his boss down.

'Fell in love first time I saw her picture,' Early remarked, his blond hair catching the sunlight, his beard and moustache neatly trimmed for the occasion. He carefully folded the catalogue page as if it was the most precious document in the world, then replaced it in his vest pocket.

Rice had never known him this way before; normally he was all hustle and bustle, rousting his men out to work long before first cockcrow, driving them and his animals with firmness, never having a second for day-dreaming.

Funny how a woman could change a man's nature, even before she met him face to face!

Rice had to agree with Seth. Gabriella's lips looked designed for kissing. She made him wish he was clever enough and rich enough to attract such a female for himself, but he figured without a hefty bank account behind him, no woman would give him a second glance. Particularly so because whenever one of those saloon females fluttered her eyelashes in his direction or commented on his tall build and other likely attributes, he became tongue-tied and clumsy. He'd always felt shy in the presence of white women though one day he was determined to pick up enough courage and do the deed with one of the dance-hall girls so he could brag like the other fellows — but he was only eighteen and maybe he'd wait a year or so.

Early had dragged out his gold watch. 'We ain't got much time,' he announced. 'Promised I'd be in town to meet Gabriella off the noon stage, but I must pick up the ring from Landry's Store before that. A weddin' day is special. I want it to be the happiest moment of her life. A fine lady like her deserves the best, that's for certain.'

'Sure,' Rice nodded, 'and I'll do all I can to make things run smooth.'

Early patted his shoulder. 'I appreciate havin' you along, kid.'

They mounted up, spurred their horses down the slope, little realizing that the next few minutes were to shatter all Seth Early's dreams . . .

★ ★ ★

The shots took them completely unaware. They'd just started down a narrow defile where high, shielding scrub covered sides that were topped with green spruce — a perfect place for an ambush. The gunfire, the sing of bullets, had Rice's chestnut horse screaming and rearing up. Rice was thrown out of the saddle, hitting the rocky ground heavily on his left shoulder. His foot was caught in the stirrup and he was dragged along ten yards of rugged ground, bumping unmercifully, before he shook free. His ears were full of gunshot echo, men shouting, and the pound of hooves as his horse high-tailed away down the defile.

Early's fine piebald had not been so lucky. It had dropped immediately, a bullet through his head. Early himself was pinned to the ground as men surged from their cover.

While Rice uncobbled his senses, rough hands grabbed the collar of his coat, dragged him into a sitting position. 'We got a big, soft giant here,' somebody cried.

He got his eyes open, realized several men were grouped around him. They were shaggy and filthy, their ragged clothing grimed with traildust, the stink of their sweat filling his nostrils. They

24

were all holding guns. He felt like a cornered bull.

He unleashed a great bawl of anger and started to struggle, but one of the attackers thrust the muzzle of his pistol forward and said, 'One more move from you, kid, and I'll blow your dawgone brains out!' He stepped back, pistol still levelled. 'Put your hands on your head!'

The young cowboy cursed, then complied, knowing that he was helpless. He sat hunched forward, his brain racing, trying to understand why this was happening. Another man, clearly Mexican, leaned down, lifted Rice's hand-gun from its holster.

The fellow covering him watched him with gimlet-eyes, his finger curled about the trigger. Rice realized that one false move on his part and that finger would tighten. He also realized that the attention of the other men had swung up the defile where there had been a scuffle. There was much cursing and shouting, and Rice could see that they had dragged Seth Early from beneath his horse and forced him to stand erect.

There were seven ambushers now in the defile, and four of them were standing around the rancher, their guns pointed. A lariat had been thrown over his head, so that his arms were pinned to his sides. He stood tight-lipped, powerless.

And then Rice heard a deep voice and noticed the big red-shirted man, powerfully muscled and heavy, who was clearly the leader of the attackers. His words carried clearly, like the pronouncement of a judge. 'Seth Early, I waited years for this moment. Now you're gonna pay for what you done to me!' And as he nodded his head, a pock-faced man threw a rope over the branch of a stunted cedar tree that stood at the crest of the defile. Its branches jutted out at crazy angles. It was the perfect hanging tree.

Early still said nothing as he was dragged up the slope to the place intended for his execution.

Rice could remain inactive no longer. There seemed little he could do to save his boss, but he had to try. The attention of the man covering him had wavered at last, his eyes drifting towards events up the defile. Rice sucked in his breath, then launched himself upward, striving to snatch the pistol. He got his hands on the weapon's barrel, forcing it aside — but the man rammed his knee into Rice's groin. They struggled fiercely, Rice trying to break free, stumbling over some large rocks. He was big and strong, might well have escaped, but two men had come rushing from the main group, and he found himself grappling against a barrier of arms. He caught one fellow across the face with his fist, sent him spinning away, but he was fighting a losing battle. Somebody grabbed him from behind, trapping his arms against his sides, dragging him back and down. Then, for a wild moment, they closed over him, the swing of their fists restricted only by limited space as they struggled to get at him. Suddenly the deep voice that had pronounced sentence on Seth Early sounded again. 'Let me do this! Let me show the bastard!'

He had stepped across, a look of intense satisfaction on his dark-bearded face. His eyes seemed almost black and were set deep under thick brows. The bones of his narrow face were prominent amid his thick beard, and his nose was high-ridged, hawk beaked. Despite his heavy build, there was something cat-like about his movements. He was holding a long-barrelled Remington. Rice felt surefire certain he was about to die. He went ice-cold. He had nothing to lose, so he started to shout at the outlaw, telling him to let Seth Early alone, that he was the kindest, most decent man who ever walked this earth.

The outlaw's lips curved downward into a cynical smile. He hefted his weapon and flicked open the loading gate. He twirled the well-oiled cylinder. He replaced a couple of spent shells. Then he closed the weapon and his finger curled around the trigger. Rice felt the gun prod his temple, saw how the man drew back his lips as if steeling himself for the gun's explosion. Rice closed his own eyes, never expecting to see Texas again — but the seconds dragged by and still he was alive. He heard men laughing, then somebody said, 'Finish off the big bastard, Vince!'

But the gun wasn't fired. When Rice opened his eyes, the barrel had been withdrawn, then it returned with brutal swiftness, cracking against his skull, dispatching him into darkness.

★ ★ ★

Bluebottles buzzed around his head. He figured a long time had elapsed. When he raised his arm to scare the flies off, he grunted with pain. His shoulder felt as if it was broken; so did his jawbone. He got his eyes open

29

and blinked at the bright, sun-stark sky above. He felt nigh cooked alive, the sun was so hot. He was lying in scrubby grass, half wedged against a slab of rock. He got some leverage against it, clawed himself up, groaning at the pain. Once on his feet, he stood swaying . . . and then the reality of what had happened hammered into him — and he wondered why he was alive. Where had his attackers gone?

He noticed Early's horse, sprawled where it had been shot. Flies had settled like a shimmering metal helmet about its brain-seeping head, and a sickening visceral smell thickened the hot air. Then he looked further up the defile and saw something that was to scar his memory for always. The body of Seth Early hung from the spruce, his bare feet dangling a yard above the ground, his ornate sixteen-inch Texas boots, especially made for his wedding, stolen. Rice stumbled across to him, foolishly hoping the whole incident was a crazy nightmare. But that hope died straight away. He could see the rancher's neck had been stre... how the rope had choked him to death. His features were contorted, his eyes bulging, wide and glassy.

Grief caught in Rice's throat, made him gag. Big tears rolled down his cheeks. He hadn't cried for anybody before, apart from his folks. Now, he couldn't help it. Maybe he'd never exactly loved Seth Early, but it was as near as you could get. He'd been a true benefactor. Now . . . ?

Angry at himself for crying, seething with black hatred for the devils who'd committed this fearful deed, he brushed away his tears.

Instinct had him groping into his coat pocket, discovering the inevitable. The wad of dollar bills intended for wedding expenses was long gone — as was his pistol.

He worked his shoulder, rubbed it, and reckoned he'd been lucky. It didn't seem broken, just bruised. He fingered his jaw, opened his mouth, satisfied himself that he could still chew, though his teeth felt a bit jagged.

It took him ten minutes to get Early down from the tree, and it was the most heartbreaking task he'd ever undertaken. He checked the rancher's pockets. He'd been carrying a lot of cash to pay for the ring and other gifts. It was all stolen. So was his fine Smith & Wesson and gold watch.

He cursed over and over and wished he still had his horse so he could chase after those killers. But he knew that on foot, in this wild country, it would be futile. They were probably miles away by now. Nevertheless, he vowed that he'd track them down soon. He'd give them a taste of their own wicked medicine — or maybe something worse. Particularly the man they'd called Vince.

He debated whether or not to bury the body, but he had no spade and the sun-baked earth was hard. Anyway, Seth's brother Able would want a proper burial with words spoken from the Bible, so, as respectfully as he could, Rice hauled Early into the shadow of the rocks and covered him with grass and stones which he hoped would discourage the flies and any other creatures that came poking around.

He thought about Gabriella Devaney. The least he could do was break the awful news to her and maybe console her in some way.

4

He found his Stetson, dusted it off and rammed it on to his head. He felt as if his whole world had caved in. The sun, cruel as a buzzard's eye, was directly overhead. Gabriella Devaney's stage must have already arrived in town. He started out on the long trudge, all the while feeling edgy in case those murderers were not as far away as he'd thought. Maybe they were regretting letting him live. Why had they? Maybe now, they were planning to dole out another dose of lead poison in his direction. It was an uncanny feeling — the suspicion that at this very moment he might be plumb centre in some fellow's rifle-sights, that he might be only seconds away from death. It made him itch, made him progress as if he was walking on eggs. But the only sound, as he progressed down the dips and ridges of that mountain, came from the whirring of grasshoppers in the grass, the only movement, apart from his own, provided by the hawk hovering on the high thermals and once he caught sight of a coyote eyeing him from the scrub, a squirrel in its jaws. He concentrated on setting one foot ahead of the other, drawing strength from his anger. Gradually the pine trees gave way to juniper, yucca and cypress. He figured the first thing he must do on reaching town was to tell the marshal what had happened.

When he made it to Bull Crossing, the sun's heat was beginning to slacken. He crossed the shallow ford as the town clock was chiming four. The town was insignificant. It didn't even have a church. Its one street was lined with stores, bank, saloon and hotel. The buildings seemed to lean against each other for support. Behind these was a straggle of weathered shacks. Activity tended to die in the afternoons when the sun was hot. Now, scarcely any folks had roused themselves from siesta. Even a big white dog, sprawling across the boardwalk, failed to raise its head as Rice stepped over it. Going directly to the marshal's office, he cursed as he found the door locked and a note pinned up saying 'Back Thursday' which was three days hence. He stood outside wondering what he should do, then he thought of Gabriella Devaney, no doubt booked into the hotel and wondering what had happened to her intended husband.

Rice was still feeling bruised and battered from the punishment he'd taken, still stunned from the shock of it all. He figured he needed some fortification before he undertook the task of enlightening Gabriella, she being a stranger to the harshness of this brutal territory.

Seth Early's killers had left a few coins in his pocket; from oversight rather than consideration, he felt sure. He stepped over to the saloon, roused the sleeping bartender. The only other activity came from a man tinkering on a piano at the back and a parrot in a cage which squawked obscenities. Rice had himself a whiskey. Then, feeling the least he could do was take the lady some sort of gift, he paid the bartender for a bunch of lilies that was adorning the end of the bar. They were past their prime, but there were no others. He hoped she'd understand.

The suit Seth Early had fitted him with seemed tighter than ever, and it was sweat-sodden with a splash of blood darkening the collar. No wonder! He'd almost died in it.

He refreshed himself in a horse-trough, sleeking back his dark hair. Somehow he felt exposed and uncomfortable with his locks trimmed short, but Seth Early had insisted he toned down his Indian appearance for the wedding, not wanting to frighten the lady. He crossed the hard-mud street and made his way apprehensively to the Lucky Strike Hotel. He'd never undertaken such a sensitive task and it weighed heavily on him. Supposing she became inconsolable at the news? Dealing with women had never been his strong point.

In the hotel lobby, a Mexican clerk was slumped over the desk. He perked up as Rice entered and looked at him disdainfully. Of course there was no guarantee that Gabriella Devaney had arrived on the stage, but when Rice said 'Miss Devaney. I need to see her,' the Mexican nodded.

'Up ze stairs, *señor*, room six. But don't barge in. She just order a bath-tub.'

Slowly he climbed the stairs, trying to form in his mind the exact words he was going to use. He wished he had fresher flowers. Finding room six, he raised his knuckles to knock and hesitated. From inside he could hear a female voice singing and the splash of water. My God, she was probably naked! He waited what seemed an age, then knocked. The singing immediately stopped. Her voice called, 'Who's there?'

His words came in a breathless mumble. 'I've come from Seth Early. I . . . ?'

'Who?'

'Mister Seth Early.'

'Where've you been, Seth?' and there was a flurry of movement inside the room, then the door was flung open and Rice got his first sight of Gabriella Devaney. The breath died in his throat. She was red-haired beautiful. For a moment neither spoke. She had a blue floral gown draped casually about her. She'd clearly just stepped from the bath, and the dampness soaked into the gown, making it cling to her curvaceous body. She looked somewhat older than the sweet-smiling girl in the picture; but that in no way reduced her bloom. She was tall for a woman, coming up to Rice's shoulder. She had a mass of russet hair and big blue eyes that matched her gown. She stared at him and there was a look of fascination, of approval, on her face.

My God, she was a good looker,

no doubt about that, and with her femininity so haphazardly concealed by the flimsy gown, Rice could feel his blood pounding, the past and the future completely overshrouded.

Suddenly she broke the ice, repeating, 'Seth . . . Seth Early. Who'd have ever thought you were so youthful,' and in a gush of warm affection she threw her arms about him and kissed his lips, then drawing back and gazing into his eyes, words tumbled out of her in the quaintest Eastern accent. 'Well . . . I thought you were never coming, Seth. But you're so much younger than I imagined . . . and bigger. Oh yes, bigger!' She laughed. 'And you look as though you've been dragged through a hedge backwards . . . but those flowers . . . so sweet of you, honey. And those lovely letters you wrote. I kept every one. I do hope you've got that wedding fixed for tomorrow. Come in so I can get a real good look at you!' And with that he was somehow sucked into the room and she'd closed the door behind him and he was enveloped by the aroma of the scented soap she'd so recently been using.

He was speechless. The gown was practically slipping off her.

She laughed again. 'My oh my, you sure do have a fine, big body, Seth Early. I'm just itching for us to get to know each other really well. I've been waiting so long.' And she unleashed a rapturous sigh, clutched him in her arms once more and pressed her warm, moist lips to his with renewed and stronger fervour, only easing back for breath.

'But you look in need of a bath — and there's that lovely tub there. You just jump in and refresh yourself.'

'But . . . '

She silenced him by laying a slim finger on his lips. 'Seth! We're going to be married tomorrow. Now's no time for false modesty! Better get yourself a new suit too. I guess you can afford it with all your money.'

He knew this was crazy, but there was

something positively marvellous about having a gorgeous woman, half naked herself, fussing over you. He had the feeling that any moment she'd be easing off his clothes, garment by garment, feigning motherly concern which, in truth, wasn't motherly at all.

'But Seth,' she went on, gazing at him with closer scrutiny. 'How come your face is all bruised?'

Sanity descended on him, and with it a mental vision of Seth Early's contorted face as he dangled at the rope's end.

'Miss Devaney . . . ' he started.

'Oh for heaven's sake, don't be so formal. Call me Gabriella.'

'Gabriella,' he said. 'There's somethin' I got to tell you.'

At first she didn't seem to hear him, just kept chattering away, but then the severe tone of his voice sank in and she stopped talking mid-sentence, maybe for the first time sensing that things weren't exactly as she'd taken them to be. 'What something.' she asked.

'On the way here,' he said, 'we got bushwhacked in the mountains . . . '

'Bushwhacked?' she queried, not knowing what the word meant but taking its definition to be 'drunk'. 'Well, I noticed the whiskey fumes hanging on your breath . . . but I guess there was no harm in a little celebration.'

'No,' he said. 'That's not what I mean. We got ambushed by outlaws. I just come to tell you Mister Early won't be available for no marriage. You see, he was killed!'

She opened her mouth to speak, but for once no words gushed forth. At last she emitted a sort of choking sound and gasped, 'You mean . . . you mean, you're not Seth Early, not . . . '

'My name's Rice Sheridan. I'm just a ranch hand at the Double Star Ranch. Mister Early's body is lyin' out there in the mountains.'

Her expression changed to stark incredulity, a disbelief of what her ears were registering. 'Seth dead? Oh no, I don't believe you. Not after I've come all this way.'

'It's true, Miss Devaney. I swear to God.'

Her face went blacker than a storm-cloud. She tried to speak but the words dammed up inside her. She became aware of her revealing position and she wrapped her gown more tightly about her and fastened the belt. 'Why didn't you tell me before?' she said at last. 'Why did you let me make a fool of myself?' There was anger building in her voice that made him flinch. Her upper lip somehow curled forward as if she was pondering deeply, then she made her decision. 'You just wait exactly where you are.' She turned away, opened the door and stepped outside. He felt uneasy about what would happen next. He felt certain it wouldn't be pleasant. He heard voices coming from down the corridor then suddenly she was back — and she wasn't alone.

Her companion was male and

intimidating. Like Rice, he had to duck as he came through the doorway. He had black hair which hung down to his shoulders and he was dressed in a fancy Eastern suit. His chin jutted out like a spade. Not knowing his profession, Rice slotted him into the category of prize fighter. He stood completely blocking any means of escape. 'That's him,' Gabriella said, her voice trembling with indignation. 'He misled me . . . Joshua, he embarrassed me!'

Her gentleman companion stepped forward aggressively, shouting, 'You had no cause to treat my sister that way!' He glared at Rice, his fists clenched. 'The Bible says it's a sin to lust after another man's wife!'

Rice could have argued that Gabriella hadn't, so far as he knew, been another man's wife, but her big, pious brother looked in no mood for discussion. In fact he reached forward, grabbed Rice's shirt-front, and began to quote more of the Bible at him. But now Rice's own ire was rising and he flailed out, pushing the other man back in surprise. Joshua stumbled over the tub, sending water splashing up like a fountain. Rice jumped across the room, thrusting Gabriella aside as she tried to intervene, suddenly sick of her charms. He went down those hotel stairs three at a time, startling the Mexican behind the counter, and a second later he was out in the street. He wondered if Gabriella's brother would come storming after him. He didn't want an outright fight with the man, but if it came to that he would not flinch.

He ran down the street, kept going for a hundred yards, then he stopped and glanced back. He breathed a relieved sigh. There was no sign of Joshua.

It was then he noticed Marshal Harry Allchurch gazing at him from the doorway of his office. He'd clearly returned earlier than his note had indicated; maybe he'd sensed there was work to be done. 'What's eatin' into you, Rice Sheridan?' he demanded.

5

Rice had always respected Allchurch. The marshal was maybe forty, but he looked older and he never touched liquor nor blasphemed. He was always instantly recognizable on account his large, blunt-ended nose. It reminded Rice of a beaver's tail. Strangely, the nose didn't render Allchurch ugly. On the contrary, he was a handsome man with a cheerful, avuncular manner, liked by all except those who broke the law. Those who came within the latter category had cause to fear him; single-handedly he'd maintained order in Bull Crossing for some fifteen years, ever since he'd quit working for the Earlys.

Now, he listened out Rice's tale of woe, his expression grim. The young cowboy related everything apart from his frolics with Gabriella. Allchurch was shaken by news of Seth Early's death, an angry twitch coming to his jaw. As he recovered from the shock, he said, 'The leader of the gang, what did he look like?'

As they entered his office, Rice described the outlaw as best he could and soon the marshal was nodding, shuffling through some Wanted notices he had in a drawer. After a moment he selected one, frowning. 'Sounds like Vince Corby, no mistake.'

'Vince . . . ' A shouted phrase slotted into Rice's memory. *'Finish off the big bastard, Vince!'*

When the marshal held up the Wanted notice, there was no doubt. The face it displayed had the familiar deep-set eyes, the beak-like nose. Rice said, 'That's him for sure.'

'Well, he sure ain't reformed none.' Allchurch scratched his nose uneasily. 'He only got released from jail six months back. It's not taken him long to stir up hell again. I'll round up some men and we'll ride up and bring Seth's body in. You better guide us to the spot, then you must ride on and warn Able. Tell him it was Vince Corby killed his brother, like he always swore he would — and I guess things won't stop there. Maybe it's too late already, but I pray to God it ain't.'

'Why did Corby want Seth Early dead?' Rice asked.

Allchurch hesitated, then said, 'Seth was responsible for capturin' Corby ten year back. He gunned down his brother. Corby always swore he'd get even, though everybody hoped that ten years in the pen would cool him off. Clearly, it hasn't.'

Rice nodded. Allchurch hurried out and within ten minutes returned accompanied by two deputies. Soon they rode out of town, Rice astride a claybank horse the marshal had loaned him.

Dusk was deepening, sending purple shadows skulking through the undergrowth, as they reached the defile where the ambush had taken place. The whole atmosphere and recollection of what had happened here plunged Rice into deep melancholy.

He located Early's body easily enough, untampered with and still hidden in the rocks where he'd left it. The marshal and his men winced at the sight of the rancher's tortured facial expression.

'A real crude job,' Allchurch commented grimly. 'Seth must've died slow, kickin' and chokin'.'

They wrapped the stiffened corpse into a blanket, then lifted it on to the back of a horse. The marshal turned to Rice and said, 'I'll get Seth's body to the undertaker's in town. You ride hell for leather for the ranch. Let Able know the news. I doubt that things'll rest as they are. You see, Corby hates Able just as much as he did Seth.'

Rice nodded, feeling too sickened for further conversation. Leaving them, he rode on up Travis Mountain, cursing the fact that this day had ever dawned, sensing that further tragedy was hanging over them.

★ ★ ★

The headquarters of the Early ranch was situated twenty miles east of the Pecos Mountains on Plum Creek, a fast-flowing stream which, bordered by a fringe of cottonwood, cut through rich, rolling meadowland that stretched away on the north side to the Travis Mountains. The ranch-house was a two-storeyed frame structure with shaded galleries and a balcony running around the first floor. It was connected by an open walkway to a building containing the kitchen and dining-room, separated from the main abode because of fire risk. The latter rooms were the domain of Lo Sang the long serving and mute Chinese cook who had nearly burned himself out of a job more than once. Nearby stood a watchtower, windmill, blacksmith's shop, and a bunkhouse. Beyond the

51

main buildings were scattered corrals, stables and wagon sheds.

Able Early was five years younger than his brother Seth, and he was afflicted by coughing sickness. His narrow shoulders were thin and hunched over his sunken chest. In view of his frail health, he had left the rugged outdoor work of the ranch to Seth, concentrating on running the office side, settling bills and organizing the paperwork. Seth had given his younger brother a free rein, allowing him to indulge his penchant — playing five-card poker. In the past, Able had always played within his means, winning as much as he lost. When Rice returned to the ranch that evening, Able was involved in a poker session with two neighbouring ranchers, Major Ed Buckley and Cres Olney — and the storekeeper from town, Scotsman Thomas McAllister. They sat about the green-baize table in a haze of cigar smoke and whiskey fumes. Caught in a losing streak, Able had just slapped his cards down in disgust, throwing in his hand. He'd gone even more pallid than usual. He kept tugging at his limp moustache, his face pained.

It was even more pained when Rice burst into the room and broke the news of Seth's death. Able said, 'Vince Corby!' Then he did the same as he always did when he was emotionally upset. He started to cough.

Thomas McAllister, the storekeeper, stubbed out his cigar and rose from the card table. He was a tall, feisty looking man whose red face was constantly blistering from the sun. He wore a monocle which he kept on a string around his neck. 'In view of these tragic circumstances,' he said, 'I think further poker is out of the question. Laddie, if you'll give me an IOU, we'll be on our way.'

Both the visiting ranchers nodded in agreement. 'With cow-thieves around, we best look to our herds,' big Cres Olney said, putting on his Stetson and coming to his feet.

Able had quieted his coughing. His narrow-chested body was trembling with the shock of losing his brother, but he steadied himself. 'I guess we've all got to look to our stock,' he said. 'I'll bid you good night, gentlemen. We'll carry on our game in a day or so.'

Despite the fact that his card-playing companions were anxious to depart, McAllister hesitated, eyeing Able in a way that Rice sensed was not entirely motivated by sympathy.

'I'm sorry to pressurize you right now, laddie,' McAllister said, 'but there's a large sum of money involved. If you could let me have your written IOU, we'll get going.'

As McAllister started to put on his gloves, Rice noticed how white, how pale, his hands were. He seemed to treat them with great care — they had not been exposed to the sun like his face.

Able had only been half listening, being deep in thoughts of his own. McAllister repeated his request. Only then did Able sigh deeply and take out a pen from the writing-desk which stood in the corner of the room. He scribbled a note, then passed it to the storekeeper who peered through his monocle, satisfying himself that it was in order. All three then stepped out into the night, and shortly the receding hoofbeats of their horses sounded.

'Corby's sure to go for the herd on the home range,' Able said, a tinge of panic showing in his voice. He hesitated, then turned to Rice and added, 'If anythin' happens to them prime cows, I'm ruined.'

Rice nodded and said, 'We best round up some men and mount extra guards out there.'

'Sure.' Able had jerked out of his uncertainty, was buckling on his six shooter. 'Go tell Brad what's happened, tell him to get the men movin'. We must pray to God we ain't too late!'

Rice hurried away to find the ranch foreman.

Within twenty minutes, Able, his thin

body hunched in a coat to offset the night's chill, a scarf pulled across his mouth, was leading a bunch of ten men out on to the star-lit range, the urgency of their pace causing the dust to stream behind them like white smoke from a locomotive. All the men were heavily armed. At Able's shoulder, Rice rode, having replaced his stolen gun with a long-barrelled, bone-handled Colt .45 that Seth Early had given him on his eighteenth birthday. He was weary after his experiences of the day, but he was determined to go after Vince Corby and avenge the killing of the man he'd respected above all others.

Perhaps Corby and his gang had left the territory, had no intention of continuing their havoc, but instinct warned Rice that this was not so.

6

The weeks prior to Seth Early's murder had seen a flurry of activity on the far-flung range. A dozen extra hands had been taken on for the spring round-up, combing some 700 square miles for the wandering animals, flushing them out from the brush and steep-sided ravines, herding them in for cutting, selected castration and branding with the double-star. As always, Rice had toiled wholeheartedly, his working garb unchanged for weeks. Like the rest, he'd become mud-caked, blood-smeared and stinking of grease, dung and smoke. But the job had been completed and, by just before Early's scheduled wedding, 1,500 cows, some of them with a horn-span of six feet, had been herded on to the home range — the grassy Cooper's Valley ten miles from the ranch-house. Here they would fatten on the lush spring verdure before being driven up the long Chisholm Trail, across the Washita and Cimarron Rivers to Abilene and the lucrative markets of the north. At least that was Seth Early's plan, but his death and the appearance of notorious cow-thieves in the territory had cast a shadow of jeopardy over everything.

As they galloped across the night range towards Cooper's Valley, desperate to thwart any mischief Corby might have in mind, Rice had the harrowing feeling that they were already too late. He wondered how Able would react now that he was without the steadying influence of his brother. Would he be strong enough to assume the overall management of the Double Star?

Able was bravely striving to take on Seth's mantle, goading the party to greater speed, but even as they rode his frail body was raked with coughing, the cold and dusty night air biting into his lungs despite the shielding scarf which covered his lips. When they stopped briefly to rest their horses, he drew close to Rice, desperation making his eyes show white in the darkness. 'My God, kid,' he murmured, keeping his voice low, 'if anything happens to that herd, if we don't get it to market, I'm ruined. I . . . ' He shook his head, his words tailing off.

'You got debts,' Rice said.

Able nodded. 'Things've got out of hand, I guess. And Corby'll ruin us if he can, one way or another. He's killed Seth, and he won't let it rest there.'

'Why's he so riled up with hate?'

Able hesitated, fighting back the cough that was rising in his chest. He pondered for a moment, then said, 'Ten year back, he hit us like he had a dozen other ranches, tried to run off our stock. But Seth and I outwitted him, set up an ambush along with some Rangers. We massacred his gang, gunned them down at their camp up on Coyote Creek. Seth and me went after Corby and his brother, cornered them in a box canyon. Seth shot Corby's brother when he poked his head up from behind a rock, blew his brains out. After that we kept Corby pinned down until the Rangers came up and captured him. He was seething mad; he didn't know whether it was Seth or me who'd killed his brother. He swore blind that both of us would suffer, that one day he'd get even with us sure as Texas. We hoped a stint in jail would cool him off.'

'But it sure hasn't,' Rice murmured grimly.

Able drew himself up, eased back his scarf and spat out a gob of phlegm. 'Let's get movin',' he said, 'and pray to God Corby ain't beaten us to it.'

They urged their horses on, the only sounds the thud of hooves, the rhythmic creak and pop of stirrup leathers, the jingle of bit-chains — and the bark of Able's coughing. As they neared Cooper's Valley, they swung southward so as to approach from downwind, fully aware that any sudden or unexpected sound, scent or movement could panic a restful herd into stampeding mania.

Cooper's Valley was a steep-sided canyon, some mile across, where the grass was lush and the herds could be contained in readiness for the drive north. As the riders topped the last ridge and gazed downward onto the moon-glazed flat, Able breathed a thankful sigh. All appeared quiet. The dark masses of silent cattle spread beneath them showed no agitation, the small glimmer of a camp-fire and the white smudge of the chuck wagon canopy revealed nothing untoward. There were eight men guarding the 1,500 cows, with the experienced trail boss Will Carver in charge. Right now, there would probably be three riders patrolling the outer fringes of the herd, a wrangler minding the remuda of horses, while the remainder rested.

Able ordered the party to dismount, and they proceeded on foot, leaving the horses in the care of one man. Rice was well familiar with the downward path, and he led the way as they stealthily descended into the valley, taking infinite care to preserve the tranquillity. Soon Rice's softest bird call gave warning of their presence, and at Will Carver's faint response they sidled into the circle of camp-fire glimmer. Able broke the news of Seth's death to Carver who for a minute was so stunned he just stood with his mouth sagged, shaking his shaggy head in disbelief. Rice had seldom seen a grown man so close to tears as Carver was then. The tough foreman had served Seth Early loyally. Now all he could do was curse over and over.

Able was determined to waste no time. He doubled the guards on the herd and stated that he wanted the herd on the move within a week, fully fattened or not.

Weariness was catching up with Rice. He wrapped himself in a blanket and snatched some rest. As he tried to sleep, tried to shrug off sombre reflections of the day's events, he was aware of a restlessness in the surrounding cows. Despite the outward appearance of calm, the beasts were not lying quietly, but often got to their feet, exchanging a moment's lowing before they bedded down again. They were more active tonight than was usual. He wondered if they somehow sensed the fear that had hastened Able and the rest of them from the ranch, somehow sensed a heaviness on the night air that augured danger. But the hours slipped away and Rice was eventually roused in the glimmer of dawn, the aroma of frying bacon, beans and coffee drawing him to his feet.

He spent the morning cruising the rims overlooking the valley, cautiously searching for sign of intruders. He rode east, following a cut-off of the valley, watching its floor rise towards the shoulder of a rocky ridge. Suddenly, he reached the brink of a cliff which dropped dizzily away into a chasm cleaved by a stream. Its rocky bed, showing but a trickle of water, was more than a hundred feet below.

Standing at the edge of the abyss, he shaded his eyes, scanning the rolling grasslands that reached into the far distance where mesas and peaks were layered against the horizon. The only movement on that vast landscape came from the sun's shimmer. Eventually he turned back.

At noon he came upon an arroyo where the rock sides narrowed inward like a bottle's neck, concealing gloomy depths. It was a secret place which he had stumbled upon a couple of years back. Now his Indian-instinct warned him that something was wrong. He tethered his black-and-white mustang to the brush, climbed down warily on foot, finding the remains of two camp-fires and thereafter indication that a group of men and horses had paused here. He touched the embers of a fire, feeling their warmth, the name of Vince Corby whispering through his head like a snake's hiss.

He was backing out, intent on carrying warning to Able, cursing that he had not picked up sign earlier, when his worst fears were realized. From behind, a gritty voice sliced through the silence. 'Stay where you are. Raise your hands!'

7

He froze, debating whether he should chance his luck and reach for his gun. But then he heard the rustle of foliage ahead and saw a man step into the open and stand with his back against the rock face. He was levelling a rifle, holding it one-handed like a pistol. He was short and bandy with a pock-marked face. It was he who'd tossed the rope over the cedar tree so they could lynch Seth Early.

With at least one gun covering him from the front and another from behind Rice had no option but to lift his arms.

'It's the damned kid,' the bandy man exclaimed. 'I s-said Vince s-should've killed him when he had the chance.' The words were slurred. Rice noticed that he had a half-empty liquor bottle in his free hand. The man was drunk;

this made him even more dangerous.

Rice heard whoever it was behind him hawk and spit, then start to snigger, finding mirth far beyond that which the situation demanded. He moved into view, a small weasel-faced fellow, with a scrawny beard and yellow protruding teeth which were exposed as he laughed. 'He'll sure be sorry he came pokin' around here.' He was aiming a pistol at Rice's head. 'Ain't nothin' stoppin' us from puttin' a bullet in him now.' Despite his apparent glee, there was no humour in his thin face, just meanness.

The other man scratched his pock-marked jaw, then said, 'Sound of the shot would carry. Vince wouldn't want that, not right now. Get a rope, tie him up.'

Weasel-face said, 'Sure,' and backed off into the trees. Rice figured he must have had his horse fairly close because he returned almost immediately, uncoiling a rope. 'Maybe we can't shoot the bastard,' he sniggered, 'but we could have our own private lynch-party. That wouldn't make much noise. There's a real nice convenient tree just up the slope.'

Again the other man pondered, then he belched, took a quick swig from the bottle and gestured towards Rice with his rifle. 'S-start climbing, kid. You s-start climbing to that tree, so's we can have a little fun.'

Rice felt certain he had only two immediate adversaries. He adopted a submissive manner, nodding in agreement, but inwardly his mind was racing swifter than a cow-pony's hooves. He had no intention of walking to a tree so they could string him up. Nor was he going to be intimidated by guns that they, for fear of Vince Corby, were reluctant to use. Why should Corby care? He concluded uneasily that the outlaws probably wanted to conceal their presence in this valley, that they intended mischief and a premature gunshot would destroy the element of surprise. Nor was the reason Corby had left these men behind difficult to fathom. They were too red-eyed drunk to be of use.

Putting on an act of clumsiness, he started to climb the slope, his path taking him up to the bandy-legged man who had only slight room to ease back against the rock face to let him pass. Reaching him, Rice erupted into action, leaping to grab hold of the rifle.

He got his hands around the barrel, forced it up, struggling to wrench it from the other man's grasp. His adversary was cursing, his bloodshot eyes bulging as he yelled at his companion to grab Rice from behind.

Still hanging on to the gun, Rice twisted, saw the weasel-faced man scrambling forward. Rice brought his foot up, bending his knee, then he straightened his leg, driving his heeled boot full tilt into Weasel's midriff. Weasel unleashed a shocked gush of wind, his eyes and gasping mouth reflecting consternation. He stepped back, clutching his belly, looked about to vomit, but instead he went down.

Meanwhile, Rice had lost his hold on the gun. The bandy man tried to draw it back and find space to level it, but Rice ducked low and got his arm around the other man's thighs, butted hard with his head and dragged him over. They rolled down the slope, first one on top then the other, the gun cast aside. They hit steeper ground and were caught in an avalanche of rocks and loose soil, both helpless to stop, and suddenly they were over the lip of the arroyo, dropping into the gloom. They fell some fifteen feet, hitting the hard-rock floor heavily, but Rice had the benefit of being on top and his fall was cushioned. He felt his solid weight crush the other man, heard him cry out as the unmistakable crack of breaking ribs sounded.

He scrambled up, wrenching his Colt. 45 from its holster, thankful that he hadn't lost it in the struggle. He thumbed back the hammer, swinging it towards the other man who lay face-down, blood trickling across the rock from the side of his head. Suddenly he emitted a groan and began to move.

Rice had no time to sympathize. A fresh deluge of pebbles cascaded downward, bouncing on his shoulders. He glanced up, saw the weasel-faced man peering over the rim, his hand-gun steadied for a shot. Rice flung himself sideways as the weapon blasted off, the bullet splintering the rock close by, its echo bouncing off the arroyo walls. He brought his own gun up, fired, but he couldn't tell if he'd achieved a hit or if the other man had simply ducked back.

Moving frantically, he clawed his way along. He knew that if either of his enemies was still active, he would be an easy target within the rocky groove. He kept glancing up towards the rim, his gun raised and ready. He followed the arroyo's twists and turns, fearing that he would be shot at. The rock-floor levelled out, then started rising.

A minute later he climbed pantingly out of the arroyo, lay in the high grass, hoping that he'd somehow got clear of his enemies. He concluded that he had, then, all at once, his relief died into insignificance because he heard a new sound: the concentrated crackle of gunfire, intermingled with the shrill cries of men — all coming from down in the valley.

Anguish cut through him. Any hope he'd cherished of getting warning to Able and the others was dashed. And as that knowledge seeped into his stunned mind, the gunfire and shouting was supplemented by an alarmed bawling and bellowing of beasts — a dreaded and ominous sound he'd heard before, most memorably up along the Red River, when the wild rush of stampede had almost cost him his life.

He came to his feet, not caring whether his immediate attackers were about or not. Glancing around, he frantically orientated himself, then scrambled through the foliage, striking up the slope. Minutes later, he found his mustang, anxiously waiting where he had tethered it in the brush. He snatched the reins free, swung into the saddle, rammed his toes into the stirrups and kicked the nervous animal into motion. They plunged down a steep escarpment at reckless pace, leaped over a crevice and then galloped up on to a sandstone promontory which commanded a view of the valley. Drawing rein, Rice gazed down and groaned.

Beneath him, the huge herd was milling, beasts piling together like logs jammed in a whirlpool, the babble of their throats reflecting terror. He could see riders racing along their flank, firing guns into the beasts. And then suddenly it was as if a thousand head had been waiting for the signal, and its impact cut through them with the speed of electric impulse. Simultaneously they were off, running with tails up and outspread horns weaving. The deafening thunder of iron-hard hooves, the awful clacking of horns, was like the breaking of an earth-shaking storm.

Across the valley, he glimpsed the white flash of the chuck wagon's canopy, raked by horns, tossed like a flapping sail in the wind as it showed above the surge of brown backs. The wagon itself stayed upright, saved only by the beasts' natural instinct to sidestep the obstruction as the sheer compactness of the mass sent them trampling through the camp-site.

He fought back his despair. He had to try and turn the herd, and pray that other Double Star riders would do the same. To achieve this it would be necessary to overtake the lead animals, bring them down or turn them and somehow get the herd to mill into a circle.

As he sent the mustang skidding down the steep gradient, the dust rose about him, gritty in his throat, making him gag. He hoisted his bandanna over his face, and rode in alongside the wild, horn-clattering current, ramming hard with his heels to keep pace with the violent rush. At any moment his mount could step into a gopher hole, send him plunging down amid the trampling hooves, but it was a chance he had to take.

He was swept along like a twig in a flood, but presently, as the valley broadened, he found space to overtake the racing beasts. He constantly glanced about for sight of other riders. Those he did glimpse amid the clouding dust and turmoil did nothing to reassure him. They were not attempting to quell the stampede, but were adding to the panic by shouting and discharging their guns, dropping beasts indiscriminately. As he pounded on, the truth grew starkly apparent. The stampede had been started intentionally — a continuation of Vince Corby's villainous scheme to ruin the Earlys and all they stood for.

Galloping parallel to the herd, he was approaching its head when he saw how the leaders had been turned off at a tangent, leading the surge up an adjoining canyon — and now the final callous element of Corby's plan became evident. Normally, the mouth of this canyon was obstructed by a barrier of rocks. This prevented beasts from ascending to the dangerous cliff-top he had climbed to earlier that day. He cried out with torment. The barrier had been removed and positioned across the main trail. Nothing beneath God's heaven would now stop the mass, driven by the pressure of those following, from plunging to destruction.

He became aware that his mustang was faltering, the surge of the animal's muscles no longer steady beneath him. They had mounted a slight hump in the ground, alongside which cows were rushing. The sharp horn of a big steer raked the lathered flank of the pony and he felt his saddle slip and knew that the girth had been severed. Almost immediately he lost his grip, helpless to prevent himself from sliding around the animal's barrel. He hit the ground amid flailing hoofs, feeling the earth's awesome tremble, rolling himself into a tight ball. With his arms wrapped about his head protectively, he surrendered himself to blind luck, expecting at any moment to be trampled into pulp. The heat generated by a thousand sweating bovine bodies engulfed him. It was akin to being broiled alive in an Indian sweat-lodge.

Eventually, hooves were no longer trampling about him. He relaxed his arms, raised his head, peered through the dust and saw how the herd was thinning, the noise diminishing. He scrambled shakily to his feet, brushing thick dust from his clothing, thankful for the second occasion within the late hour that fate had favoured him. But he felt little joy because he knew by now that hundreds of cows could have plunged to death over the high cliff and he had achieved nothing in his frantic attempt to stave off disaster.

The dust was settling and he could see across the valley, see distant riders moving about. He heard the snap of gunfire. They seemed to be taking a fiendish delight in despatching animals. Rice had little doubt that he would receive the same treatment if they discovered his presence.

The main herd had taken the turn-off, but numerous animals, trampled to death or injured, or felled by Corby's slaughterers, littered the ground. His own mustang was far gone.

Seeing the futility of remaining where he was, he decided that he'd best start the long walk back to the camp-site and discover if Able Early and any of the others still survived.

It was as he took a last glance at the now silent entrance to the side-valley, that he saw the single man astride a big bay horse riding slowly across the undulating ground, gesticulating towards his men to re-form. The rider was red-shirted, and even at thirty yards, the thick-muscled bulk of his shoulders, the cat-like, supple ease with which he sat his saddle, left no doubt as to his identity.

Rice slid his Colt from its holster, recharged the cylinder with bullets from his belt and thumbed back the hammer. His attempt to avert disaster had proved fruitless. Now there was one duty that lay within his power. That duty was to kill the man who seemed to epitomize everything that was evil in the young cowboy's mind, the man he hated beyond all others — Vince Corby.

Rice Sheridan was not a man to take killing lightly. He had been hurt too deeply himself to snuff out life without hesitation. Even so he now paced forward, gun raised, finger curled about the trigger, the desire for vengeance focusing his every sense on what he had to do. Corby had reined in, had turned his red-shirted back, apparently taken unaware as the young cowboy pulled up just a few feet behind him and called his name. Corby twisted in his saddle sharply, then seemed to relax, making a point of keeping his hand well clear of the hardware at his hip. 'The kid,' he said softly.

'Go for your gun,' Rice demanded. 'Go for your gun so's I can kill you fair and square.'

A cynical smile touched Corby's bearded face, his deep-set eyes narrowing to slits. 'Ain't no cause for ill-feelin'. Not between you and me.'

'If you won't draw on me,' Rice countered, 'I'll count to three — then I'll kill you, Corby — and I'll have no more regrets than you did when you strung up Seth Early!'

Corby gave him a contemptuous glare, then he shrugged his shoulders dismissively, turned his back and nudged his bay-horse away.

Rice kept his gun aimed, started to count . . . 'One, two . . . '

Not even an Indian could have moved faster than the outlaw did right then. Rice got his shot off, but the bullet merely cleaved space where the man had been. Corby had shielded himself on the far side of his horse. Clawing his gun from his holster, he fired from beneath his body. The bay reared, the shot went low. Rice felt the slam of impact just above his knee, but amazingly no initial pain. Instead he felt as if his leg had been blasted away and he fell, the .45 slipping from his grasp. Seconds later, raising his head, he saw that Corby was back in the saddle, was galloping away.

Glancing down, he saw that blood was soaking his Levis. He knew he'd been hit badly — and in sudden confirmation the pain struck him. Its razor-like sharpness made him cry out. He tried to get up but fell back, cursing to high heaven, never having known such agony. He tried to draw breath but somehow couldn't. Groaning, he lay upon the grass, knowing that his blood was pouring out, that he was utterly helpless and had been completely outwitted. He jerked twice, fighting his agony, fighting the white mist of giddiness rising in his brain, sensing that it might be death, then he lost consciousness.

His awareness returned. It was much

later. For a moment he drifted in a suspended cloud of vagueness, then he heard the fierce buzz of bluebottles about his leg. As he struggled to fan them away, the agony returned and with it the stark realization that he'd been left to die. He sensed he wouldn't be able to stand the agony for long and wished he could leave it all behind, slip again into oblivion. But he didn't, and he could see the paling sky above him and hear the raucous cries of buzzards squabbling over the cow carcasses that dotted the ground.

He felt strangely cold, strangely numb apart from the agony of his leg. He started to shake.

Then he heard the faint clink of movement off to his left. Somehow he raised his head, not knowing whether it was failing evening light or the blurring of his vision that handicapped his eyes. Even so he recognized the familiar red shirt of the man riding toward him. He found the strength to feel around, grunting in satisfaction as his hand settled over his gun. He sank down, hugging the concealing ground as the other man approached. Perhaps there was yet time to settle scores. Now there would be no hesitation.

8

In all his years working with cattle, ranch foreman Brad Silvers had not known such misery. First of all had come the hideous news of Seth Early's murder, then the confusion of the attack when Corby's marauders had charged into the valley, guns blazing, shooting down two loyal ranch-hands before they knew what was happening — and then the stampede.

Silvers had followed the trail left by the wayward herd, had seen the countless animals that had either been shot or trampled to death. Tracks showed that most of the herd had blundered up the side canyon — but some had been allowed to continue through a small break in the barrier across the main valley. He'd climbed to the cliff top, his heart sinking as he suspected the worst. When he gazed downward into the abyss, the horror was confirmed and made him slump to the ground, bury his distraught face in his hands. Hundreds of beasts had surged over the edge, had crashed into the depths to be crushed by those which followed. They lay in heaps on the rocks at the base of the cliffs; some had survived to hobble and thresh on broken legs. Already the ever vigilant buzzards were arriving in swarms, ripping at the flesh of dead animals.

Thank God, he thought, thank God that Able never saw this. It would have killed him. Of course that would have delighted Vince Corby. Silvers had no doubt that the outlaw would still try to keep his vow to completely destroy the Earlys and everything they stood for. But right now the foreman suspected that Corby was driving the cows he'd allowed to survive southward into Mexico. Once across the Rio Grande these would be sold at some profit — enough to pay his gang and keep them happy until it was time to return, to finish the job he'd so callously started.

Descending once more to the valley, his heart in his boots, Silvers wondered if Able had made it back to the ranch safely. The sheer catastrophe of events had left the rancher more ill than he'd been for some time, he'd drawn the dust into his failing lungs, blood had frothed to his lips as he coughed. There was nothing he could do in that state, and Silvers had persuaded him to take the chuck wagon and return to the Double Star. Two of the surviving hands had gone with him.

Silvers felt guilty for what had happened. Why hadn't he realized that most of the men he was taking into employ for the round-up were members of Corby's gang, that it was all part of the outlaw's evil plan? But he'd never suspected any trouble; never even known that a man so consumed with hatred and lust for vengeance had been released from jail. The Earlys had spoken only fleetingly of the rustler they'd once wounded and kept pinned down until the Rangers pounded in.

Silvers knew that there was little he could do here, particularly as soon the light would fade. He must return to the Double Star and discuss the future with Able. The whole outlook was grim.

As he turned his horse homeward, his broodings dulled his alertness. With, he suspected, Corby and his gang long gone, and a funereal silence hanging across the valley, he was not thinking of possible danger. Nor was he attaching the remotest significance to the fact that his shirt was red — the same colour as that worn by the outlaw leader. But it was this that placed his life in jeopardy.

The malevolent crack of the shot cut through the silence, the bullet whining close. With his horse rearing, he reacted by throwing himself free from his saddle and flattening himself against the ground in case another shot followed. But after the discharge had died in his ears, there was silence and he cautiously raised his head. It was then he saw Rice Sheridan, propped swayingly on his elbows, heard his tormented murmuring. Suddenly the young cowboy allowed the gun to slip from his fingers and slumped sideways.

Satisfied he was no longer a target, Silvers clambered up and crossed the intervening ground. He found Rice in a sorry state, his breathing shallow, his skin an awful pallor and thick with dust-grimed sweat. Blood was seeping from his leg.

Rice was hovering on the edge of consciousness, but he managed a brief whisper . . . '*Thought you was Corby.*'

He went suddenly still — and for a moment Silvers thought he was dead, but shortly he saw slight movement in his chest and knew that if Rice Sheridan was to stand any chance of survival, he must strap him across his horse and ride for Doc Finnegan's at Bull Crossing.

★ ★ ★

It was a week later. Once again Rice had drifted out of the laudanum-induced haze, his mind experiencing a moment of rare clarity. 'Is he here?' he murmured anxiously. 'Has Sabine come to cut my leg off?'

Maggie had been adjusting the wick of the oil lamp. She moved to his bedside with that quick, attentive way she had, and in the glimmering light her eyes appeared big and depthless black. Gently, she rested her hand on his. 'No,' she said. 'It's evening. He won't be here till tomorrow.'

He gazed up at her. He noticed that she was wearing a pink blouse with flowers neatly embroidered down its front. She'd tied back her dark hair with pink ribbon.

'Maggie,' he said with startling harshness in his voice, 'I don't think I can go through with it. The Comanches never tolerated a man who wasn't . . . whole. I'd rather they let me die.'

She drew in a breath sharply. 'No, Rice! Just remember you weren't born an Indian, so their rules don't apply.' Her fierce intensity shocked him. 'You won't die. You're strong and healthy and whatever happens you'll pull through. I know you will.'

'How can you be so sure?'

A defiant smile widened her lips. 'Because, Rice Sheridan, you're the bravest man I ever knew.'

'Oh Maggie . . . ' He felt blood surge into his cheeks. He hesitated, not knowing what to say. In his confusion, he asked something that had perplexed him, something in truth that was irrelevant, yet had assumed importance in his mind. 'Why is your name Maggie? I never heard that name before.'

She laughed — a gentle sound like water cascading over smooth pebbles. 'Maggie is short for Magdalen. There was a woman called Mary Magdalen in the Bible. I guess I was named after her.'

'Magdalen,' he murmured. 'That's a beautiful name. You must be awful good to be named after somebody from the Bible.' He hesitated, then asked, 'Can I call you Magdalen?'

'Oh Rice, I would like that. I really would.'

'And can I ask you another question?'

'Sure you can.'

'How come you took Seamus Finnegan for your husband?'

She smiled wistfully, dropping her voice to the faintest whisper. 'Catalogue bride.'

For a moment neither of them spoke then suddenly the pain in his leg seemed to stir, making him catch his breath. The power of the opiates had receded. Within seconds, the pain changed to throbbing agony, white hot, bringing tears to his eyes. Maggie leaned over him. 'Rice,' she murmured. 'Rice . . . let me help you.' And she eased the blanket back from his tortured limb. Finnegan had decided that it served no purpose to constrict the wound in any way and had left it only lightly bandaged with a flimsy cotton.

'Magdalen . . . ' Rice groaned, 'what're you doin'?'

'Lie back . . . relax . . . say: 'I am strong. I want to get better'.'

'Jesus . . . '

'Say it, Rice!'

So he did, murmuring the words over and over, and at the same time he felt her hands touch his knee, felt their warmth easing into him, somehow absorbing the agony so that relief spread through him and suddenly he seemed enveloped by a golden, soothing feeling that he couldn't understand.

'You *are* strong,' she emphasized, 'and you *will* get better, Rice. You'll get better . . . for me!'

'For you?'

He had thought her shy. Now he realized that beneath the apparent reserve was a strange timeless maturity, a mysterious female power. It was as potent as anything the Comanche shamans possessed. And as the minutes drifted by, her healing touch and soft voice calmed him. He basked in an inner glow, and seemed lifted to a level beyond his own body. Here, he found no pain, no fear, only deep, solacing sleep.

★ ★ ★

Just after ten on the following morning, Army Contract-Surgeon Arnold Sabine rode in from Fort Lovell. Rice was still asleep as the medical man examined the wound. He gave his head a melancholy shake and murmured the word, 'Septicaemia. I'll have to act quickly. I'll need plenty of boiling water.'

Sabine was tall and silver-haired, and in his long black coat he looked more like an undertaker than a surgeon. A deep scar decorated his left cheek where a Union Minié ball had ploughed a jagged furrow.

Like Finnegan, he was contemplating retirement shortly, though he still drew great satisfaction from his work, particularly so as at least half of his patients had survived the surgery and recovered to live normal lives, albeit with the aid of wooden limbs. But Sabine was also a man who liked to experiment. On several occasions this had been at the expense of those under his knife.

Now he unpacked his surgical bag, took out a large bottle of carbolic acid that he would use on the wound, then he carefully laid out his instruments on the side table. He had two fine bone saws, assorted knives and a selection of choppers, forceps, scalpels, clamps, probes and hooks. All were well worn but clean — so different from the bloodstained, rusty instruments he had been obliged to use for amputations on the battlefield.

During the war, there had been no time for the small luxury he today enjoyed with his old friend Seamus Finnegan — a glass of good whiskey before he got down to work. Having tipped the liquor back, he wiped his lips and said, 'This kid. What does he want done with the leg afterwards?'

Finnegan looked mournful. 'He wants it put in a child's coffin and buried alongside his boss Seth Early.'

The surgeon nodded, then he removed his black coat, put on his apron and rolled up his sleeves, suddenly showing a brisk and businesslike manner. 'Did you boil that water? We've got to steam a half-dozen towels so red-hot you can't touch 'em. We'll pack 'em around the leg.'

Finnegan nodded, was leaving the room when Maggie stepped in. She'd been sitting with Rice in the next room. Her face was pale and lack of rest had left shadows beneath her eyes. 'He's fast asleep,' she said. 'I pray the laudanum'll keep him that way.' Then she faced Sabine and added, 'Before you amputate, will you probe the wound, just to make sure . . . ?'

Impatience showed in Sabine. He resented being told how to do his job. 'No point, young lady!'

9

'I know these are bad times for you, laddie,' Thomas McAllister said, the redness of his face growing even more pronounced as his temper rose, 'but a lot o' money is involved and I won it fair and square.'

Able Early was slumped in a swivel chair behind his desk, his shoulders hunched over his narrow chest. Being a sick man, the events of the last ten days had nigh destroyed him. Right now his thin hand had opened the desk drawer in front of him, had slipped inside to fondle the butt of the Navy Colt resting there. 'Thomas,' he said, trying to keep his voice steady, 'I've lost the herd. Everythin' depended on sellin' that beef. It was the very best of what we had . . .'

'I know all that!' McAllister snapped. He started to pace up and down like an

96

exasperated schoolteacher, the monocle swinging from his neck. 'Don't count on my tears, laddie! Maybe your cows have gone, but you've still got the ranch, the land. You can still pay me off and have a bit left over.'

Able's misery seemed to overwhelm him. He was about to speak but an attack of coughing suddenly erupted from his lungs. McAllister grew increasingly impatient as he waited for the bout to finish. Before it did, he rammed on his Stetson. 'I'm not going to hang around here any longer, Able. I've got my own work to do . . . but you just remember; I won't rest till I've got every last cent of what you owe me. Understand?'

Able didn't respond, but hatred flared from his eyes as the Scotsman turned on his heel and stomped out.

After he'd gone, Able removed the gun from the drawer and laid it upon the desk in front of him. His breathing was shallow, like the pant of a dog, and sweat was beading out on his brow.

He figured he'd had as much as he could take. Maybe it would be best if he was laid to rest alongside Seth and the two ranch-hands in the Bull Crossing cemetery.

Already he was missing his brother badly — his know-how, his strength — and the lung-sickness was driving him crazy.

The knowledge that two of his men had been shot down by Corby, and that the herd was gone, many of the animals rotting to death at the base of that cliff, felt like a crushing weight pressing down on his already stooped shoulders.

Of course he couldn't really blame Brad Silvers, but he was angry with him nonetheless for taking half-a-dozen outlaws on to the pay-roll. He should have been more vigilant.

And he couldn't count on Rice Sheridan any more. If he survived having his leg amputated, he'd be finished for ranch work. Rice Sheridan . . . thought of the young cowboy made him shudder. Having him around all these years had been a constant reminder of long ago events that were locked in his mind. Perhaps half of the guilt had died with Seth . . . but that didn't make what he bore any easier to live with, didn't make his nightmares any less vivid. He forced his thoughts away from Rice.

The Double Star workforce had been slashed. Able had scarcely enough men to ride the lines and comb the range for strays and mavericks, and with the other ranches in the territory involved in round-up, all available hands had been signed on. Those he did have were busy searching for the few cows the earlier round-up had missed — and Able was alarmingly aware that there was nobody to guard the ranch-house. Apart from himself, Brad Silvers, the Chinese cook and a few others, it was deserted. Should Vince Corby return, he would easily crush any feeble resistance.

Now, to rub salt into the wound, Thomas McAllister was getting really mean, even aggressive, over the gambling debt. Like a dog worrying a stricken sheep, he would never give up.

Able surrendered to despair. I've had enough, he thought. I'd be better off dead.

He made his decision quite suddenly. He straightened up, took hold of the gun, rose from his chair and walked to the window. One last glimpse, he told himself, one last glimpse of the prairie, of the hills, of the twisting creek, the distant blue crags of the Travis Mountains . . . the land was so majestic that even in these intended final moments of his life, he stared at it for a solid minute, humbled by the voice of silence. Finally he nodded as if in farewell, his mind set on what he must do. McAllister would have everything, damn him!

Able touched the gun to his temple, felt the cold hardness of the barrel, even caressed the trigger with his finger.

Then he heard the blowing of a horse, the thump of approaching hooves, the creak of a wagon pulling into the yard. He hesitated, lowered the gun. He moved across to the other window so he could see better.

The couple climbing down from the light buckboard were strangers to him. The woman was closing her parasol. She was wearing a spectacular feather hat and a fine blue dress layered back to a bustle. Her companion was tall and brawny, and his smart eastern suit and a bowler hat did not detract from the fact that he might have looked more at home in a prize fight.

Puzzlement quirked Able. Still holding the gun, he walked out on to the veranda — and straight away she stepped towards him, a smile upon her lips.' You must be Able,' she said. 'Able Early.'

'I am,' he nodded. He wasn't used to women being so forward, so downright gushing. In fact he wasn't used to women at all. Nonetheless he gathered his wits, reached out and shook the hands of both visitors.

'My brother Joshua and I were just passing by,' she was saying, 'and we thought it would only be Christian to call and express our heartfelt condolences for all the awful tragedies that have happened. My name's Gabriella Devaney, and I came West to marry poor Seth. I'm really sorry for the way things have turned out.'

Able knew he had to be hospitable but he was self-conscious. Domestic matters had lapsed of late. The house was downright untidy, hardly the place to entertain a couple of refined Easterners like these. And this woman: he had never figured a female could look so beautiful, with her graceful posture, her rich auburn hair, her confident blue eyes that gazed into his all the while she was talking. That was why, as she turned slightly, it came as a shock to see her sway slightly, to stumble, to realize that she wasn't some goddess but was human after all. Her brother sprang forward immediately, reaching out to support her. She straightened up, hand raised to her forehead, her poise restored. 'Oh my, it must be the heat that got to me, and that bumpy ride along the trail.'

Able remembered his manners. 'You'd better come in, sit down and have a drink.'

'That would be greatly appreciated,' Gabriella smiled, her glance quickly taking in the fine ranch-house.

Within minutes they were all seated in the main room and Lo Sang had rustled up coffee and some flapjack biscuits which, imagining that the visitors were high-bred folk, he served on an old silver tray. As he departed, Gabriella said, 'That Chinaman is so respectful. Never says a word out of place.'

'He never says a word at all,' Able explained. 'He's been dumb since the day he was born.'

Able couldn't take his eyes off Gabriella. She seemed to overwhelm everything with her warm personality, not standing on ceremony like most strangers did, nor treating him like the sickly, puny individual he was. She seemed deeply hurt by Seth's death, almost as if she'd known him life long. Saying how she just knew he'd been a good man, and how much she'd wanted to be his wife, and as she spoke she dabbed her eyes with her handkerchief. She showed great interest in the ranch and how the Earlys had built their spread over the years. Reluctant to spoil the moment, Able didn't mention that he was up to his ears in debt and that the future of the Double Star was in jeopardy; nor did he comment upon the fact that seconds before their arrival he had stood with the muzzle of a gun pressed against his head. Now he was concluding that life still held some pleasure — particularly that of enjoying the charms of such a woman. As for her brother, Able hardly noticed him, for he sat silently, his attention centred on his sister.

Able was embarrassed by the dirty

dishes on the table, unwashed clothes and boots scattered on the floor. Gabriella seemed to take it all in her stride, not mocking him but comforting him. 'I guess you lack a woman's touch here, Able. Could I offer to help you, maybe get things in apple-pie order again?'

'Oh no, not in your fine dress and all, Miss Devaney . . . '

'Oh, do call me Gabriella — and Joshua and I wouldn't mind at all tidying house for you. In fact it would be an honour.'

'Well . . . well, that's real kind. Maybe you could stop here overnight. That's if you got your things.'

'As a matter of fact,' she said, 'we've got our bags in the wagon. I'll put on my apron.'

★ ★ ★

That night Able saw his guests to their rooms along the landing, rooms that had stood empty for so long, then he went to his own freshly made bed. He was amazed at the way this woman had buckled into the housework and lifted his spirits. Unbeknowingly, she had saved his life and somehow given him determination to face the future.

Despite his comforting naivety, he was unable to sleep that night. Memories haunted him — and Rice Sheridan kept probing into his thoughts. He wondered if the young cowboy would die under the surgeon's knife, and take with him reminders of events which had tortured Able's conscience down the years — and had afflicted his brother Seth with such agonizing remorse that he had constantly prayed for forgiveness and, right up to his dying day, striven to make amends to the young Rice who knew nothing of the guilt which plagued the owners of the Double Star.

10

The faces of Arnold Sabine and Seamus Finnegan appeared above him like the garish figureheads of old ships looming through moist tentacles of fog. In that dreamy, drifting world where everything echoed, he was a floating observer not a participant. He could hear the clink of instruments, even the laboured breathing of Sabine, sometimes held back as he concentrated on particularly intricate aspects of his work. And shortly Rice caught his wry comment: 'If he gets himself shot again, he best make sure the bullet hits the same place.'

'Same place?' Finnegan's voice came.

'Sure. Wood may splinter, but it won't hurt, that's for certain.'

Rice groaned.

'Give him another drop of laudanum,' Sabine instructed. 'I once knew a surgeon who got his jaw broken by an ungrateful patient.'

Soon the young cowboy had embarked on his renewed voyage into a Stygian world of indifference.

* * *

The two had sobered somewhat since their humiliating clash with Rice Sheridan before the stampede. Charlie Rawlins, the short, bandy man with the pock-marked face, was constantly complaining of his cracked ribs and the inconsiderate way in which Rice had fallen on top of him. Shortly afterward, Billy Teevis, his weasel-faced companion, had had the lobe of his left ear excised by the young cowboy's bullet. Both men were of the mean, cow-bum stock that drifted through Texas, scrounging enough money to keep them in liquor and one step ahead of the law. And neither forgot a grudge. Both had rejoined the main gang feeling sickened at being outwitted, but shame kept them tight-lipped about their galling experience.

In the days following the stampede, Vince Corby and his men had hazed what cattle they had retained southward through semi-arid country. They reached a creek and followed it towards the Rio Grande. The longhorns were hardy and nimble and accepted the relentless pace without the constant need to stop for water. Corby sensed that there was little chance of the law pursuing them, but he moved quickly, constantly having his drag-riders scan the back-trail, taking no chances. Once he reached Mexico he would sell the beef off at four dollars a head.

Before fording the Big Muddy, he sent for Rawlins and Teevis and said he had an important task for them. 'Go back to the Double Star, spy out on the place, find out if Able Early's still around. If he is, come back to me hell for leather. Don't let Early see you, don't harm him. That's a pleasure I'm savin' for myself. Understand!'

The two nodded. Corby wasn't the sort of fellow anybody crossed — and they'd already stretched his patience by getting drunk just before the attack of Cooper's Valley.

As they rode northward again, Charlie Rawlins pressed a restraining hand against his painful ribs and remarked, 'Sure enough we'll save Able Early for Vince, but there's another little matter I'm itchin' to attend to.'

Teevis glanced at his companion, his lips curling back from yellow teeth in a wolfish, knowing grin. This was the first good humour he'd shown since his ear had been shot away. 'Sure reckon I know what that is, Charlie. Guess I share the exact-same sentiment.'

Rawlins said, 'Let's go find the kid. Let's make sure he don't go hurtin' folks no more.'

They spurred their animals forward with fresh fervour.

Three days later the two outlaws reached Bull Crossing at eleven o'clock in the sun-hot morning, their insignificant appearance attracting little attention from the townsfolk. They dismounted, hitching their horses, and entered the saloon. Teevis casually enquired if the bartender had any knowledge of the tall, young, Indian-looking cowboy who worked for the Earlys.

The bartender opened two bottles of liquor and pushed them across the counter, always suspicious of strangers asking questions. 'What's it to you?'

Teevis gave his most ingratiating, yellow-toothed smile. 'We're old friends of his, anxious to renew acquaintance.'

The bartender shrugged and took him at his word. 'I guess you mean Rice Sheridan. He ain't in too good shape at present. He's across at Doc Finnegan's undergoin' treatment.'

'Treatment?' Teevis nodded his thanks. He and Rawlins downed their whiskey, stepped outside, sought directions from a passer-by, then drifted along the street towards the doctor's establishment, feigning indifference yet inwardly driven by a wolf-like tenacity. Both were sweating from the day's rising heat.

'If that poor young cowboy's being doctored,' Rawlins murmured, 'he may not feel up to arguin' as we fill him with lead.'

Both men laughed and loosened their holstered weapons.

* * *

Shocked, Maggie heard booted footsteps, pounding up the stairs. Rushing to the landing, she was confronted by the two intruders — mean-faced men with their guns drawn. She cried out in alarm, 'What do you want? You've no right to come barging up!'

Rawlins glanced at her lecherously, his bloodshot eyes stripping her naked, then he stepped forward. 'Ain't no concern of yours, Miss Pretty-Tits!' And with that he grasped her shoulder, his grimy hand soiling her pink blouse.

He paused to leer into her appalled face, then pushed her ruthlessly aside, sending her down on to the boards. Both outlaws moved into the outer room. Finding it empty, they forced open the door on its far side and blundered through. They were immediately assailed by the all-persuasive reek of carbolic.

The sight which greeted them was akin to a gawkish nightmare. The sheet-covered patient was stretched prostrate on a table. Sabine and Finnegan, clad in blood-splashed aprons, were poised over him, their alarmed faces blazing indignation at the intruders, their mouths sagging in astonishment as they found themselves covered by hand-guns. Sabine shouted, 'What in all hell . . . !' But Rawlins' snarl cut across him.

'We come for Rice Sheridan!'

'For God's sake,' Finnegan shouted, 'he's undergoing surgery . . . he's . . . '

Rawlins' ears were deaf to reasoning. He paced forward, levelled his pistol at the unconscious cowboy, would have pressed the trigger. Instead he jerked from a sudden, thudding impact. He glanced down with horrified eyes, saw the fine-honed blade of Sabine's scalpel protruding from his chest. He unleashed a choking, gurgling sound, stood nonplussed for a second, then his legs crumpled and he dropped, thumping down on the boards so heavily that the surgical instruments on the side table rattled.

Teevis, crouching just a few feet behind, gazed with wide eyes at his fallen companion, then his gaze lifted to the furious surgeon, saw him reaching for a second scalpel. Panic seized the weevil-faced outlaw; even so, he would have discharged his Colt had not Maggie hurled herself at his back, knocking him off balance, clawing his neck and shoulder with the blind frenzy of a cat. The overall effect was too great. Teevis shrugged the girl off, then twisted round, blundered through the outer room and half fell down the stairway. Maggie glanced through a window, got a glimpse of him as he ran down the street to the saloon, vaulted on to his horse. Soon the dust was clouding up and she knew he was gone.

Arnold Sabine had backed against the wall, breathing heavily, shaken by events. Finnegan stooped down to examine the fallen Rawlins. He retrieved the embedded scalpel, noting how it had pierced the heart. The diagnosis was instantaneous. 'He won't trouble us no more. That was the neatest bit of surgery you done for some time, Arnold.' He then glanced at Maggie. 'You best go tell the marshal what's happened. We don't want no misunderstanding about our reasons for annihilating this scum. There might even be a reward in it.'

Sabine was recovering his composure. Many a man had died under his scalpel, but none in the same way as this intruder.

Maggie was still trembling with shock. Her attention swung to Rice who was again stirring on the table, his low groan indicating that only seconds had separated him from being aware of the traumatic circumstances. 'His leg,' she gasped. 'Is it . . . ?'

Sabine held up a palm to calm the girl. Reaching across to a tin bowl, he extracted a small and mangled piece of lead around which a fragment of cloth was still wrapped. 'You're a very persuasive young lady, Maggie Finnegan,' he said. 'But I was going to probe into the wound before amputating, anyway. You see a surgeon doesn't take kindly to being told how to do his job. It's not the first gunshot wound I've handled.'

'His leg?' she persisted, exasperation growing in her voice.

'Bullet was embedded so deep,' Finnegan cut in. 'It'd taken a bit of his Levis with it and all gone as mouldy as sin. A less capable surgeon would never have reached it. It'd compromised his entire blood circulation, caused the infection.'

'So you haven't amputated?' she cried.

Finnegan had moved over to Rice, was attending to the dressing.

'I'm not saying he'll keep that leg,' Sabine explained. 'We'll let it drain for a few days. It may still turn bad and have to come off, and . . . '

Thank God! Maggie's hazel eyes were swimming with tears of joy. She tried to speak but emotion rose in her chokingly and all she could do was nod while a voice inside her cried out: *He's going to get better. I'll see to that!*

★ ★ ★

'You're still a whole man. You've still got your leg.' It was a half-hour later. She bent over him, her hand grasping his as he reached towards her. He made no acknowledgement, so she emphasized the point. 'Sabine didn't cut your leg off. Instead he's dug a great hole, got the bullet out, swabbed away the poison . . . '

117

He sighed, pursed his lips ponderingly, then gave his head a slow nod.

She felt suddenly impatient. 'God, Rice Sheridan! I didn't expect you to get up and dance round the room, but I reckoned you'd be pleased!'

Again the nod — and then a dreamy, satisfied smile spread across his face and only just audibly he whispered, 'Magdalen.' His eyelids drooped. His breathing settled into an easy rhythm and he drifted into sleep.

She felt exhausted herself. A man had died before her eyes, she had fought another as he aimed his gun, and finally Sabine had blessed her ears with the result of his surgery — news that came sweeter than all the harps in Heaven. It had been a day she'd remember for the rest of her life.

She adjusted Rice's bedclothes, gazed at him for a moment, then leaned forward and touched her lips to his cheek before rising to draw the curtains and slip reluctantly away.

11

Big nosed Harry Allchurch, marshal of Bull Crossing, took little comfort from the fact that violence had flared within his domain and was over before he'd been aware of the threat. Afterwards, he'd helped Seamus Finnegan carry the body of the dead man from the surgery to the shack which the doctor used as store-house and occasional mortuary. He'd then contacted the undertaker before telegraphing the county seat with news of events. Allchurch knew Charlie Rawlins of old, knew there would be few tears shed over his demise.

Now the marshal sat in his office, fingering the telegraph he'd just received from Texas Ranger Bigfoot Wallace. *Telegraph me direct if Vince Corby again shows up in the territory. Can have a company of Rangers with you in under twenty-four hours. We want him real bad.*

Allchurch put down the flimsy telegraph paper on his desk. Mention of Vince Corby caused deep-rooted uneasiness to tug at him. For years he'd forced his past into the background like a bad, best-forgotten dream. He had taken comfort in the hope that various elements would never come together, would remain like lost pieces from a jigsaw, so that the entire picture was never formed. For years, neither he nor the Earlys had spoken about what had happened. On occasions he wondered if the Earlys were tortured the same way he was, or had they dissociated themselves from events because they were too sickening to contemplate? Admittedly Seth was now beyond the reckoning, could not speak from his grave, but with Corby again on the prod, and Rice Sheridan surviving his surgery, Allchurch had the awesome suspicion that matters would not rest, that sooner or later the truth would emerge, as deadly as a snake's dry-bone rattle, to shatter the image he cherished — that of the community's God-fearing and much respected peace officer.

★ ★ ★

On the afternoon of the following day, Rice was sufficiently recovered to sit up in a chair and take notice of the world about him. His leg still throbbed painfully and just looking down made him grimace for it was not a pretty sight. Finnegan had insisted that the wound be left open to the fresh air, allowing the poison to drain out of it. Sabine had cut a great deal of rotten flesh away leaving a large hole, but at least what remained looked raw-meat healthy. However the surgeon was by no means confident that all would be well. As he'd departed for his military duties at Fort Lovell, acknowledging the young cowboy's gratitude with a smile, he'd stressed that he'd return to complete the amputation should matters deteriorate — but Rice inwardly

121

swore, come hell or high water, that would never happen, that he was going to shrug off this wretched experience and return to normal activity — an assumption that was wholeheartedly supported by the happy-faced Maggie who cared for him constantly.

He leaned back, content to watch as she moved about the room, efficiently attending to small chores. Once, when she came close, he noticed how her eyes were the colour of brown-green sage shot through with flecks of sunlight. Sometimes she stood at the window, her back turned as she gazed down into the street, as if to satisfy herself that nothing untoward would disturb the convalescence of her patient. Such moments pleasured him because he imagined that she would be unaware of the joy he took in gazing at her trim back and hips, the neat buttons that fastened her calico dress, disappearing beneath the down-sweep of her dark hair, the pinkness of her ribbon and that mysterious, wonderful womanliness that made him ache and temporarily forget that she was another man's wife.

In the evening, after Doc Finnegan had cleansed the wound and changed the dressing, Rice went back to his bed. He was feeling better and his strength was returning. Maggie came and sat beside him, some sewing in her hands. Although they weren't touching, he could somehow feel her closeness, her warmth, as if it were a solid thing. He watched her slim, tanned hands working efficiently, sewing buttons on her husband's shirts. He felt he wanted to open his heart to her, tell her how desperately he loved her — yet he knew he must not. Instead, he said: 'You're not from Texas, are you?'

She smiled, shook her head. 'Born in Boston. Father was in the Army, took me and Mother to Fort Phil Kearny on the Bozeman Trail. You've heard of Fort Phil Kearny?'

'No,' he said, feeling embarrassed by his ignorance.

'Well, in Christmas '66, the Sioux Indians mounted an attack, killed a lot of soldiers. Father was with a Captain Fetterman when his command was annihilated.'

'He was killed — your pa?'

She nodded.

'I'm sorry, Magdalen.'

'Afterwards, Mother and I went back to Boston. I was twelve then. Mother had this strange power in her hands. She could cure people of sickness. But she couldn't cure herself. She caught diphtheria and died. It was awful. I went to live with my aunt and uncle. Aunt Beth tried to be kind, but my uncle Bob . . . he . . . ' She paused, emotion rising in her, then she went on: 'I've got a scar across my back where he hit me. I couldn't stand him any longer. I ran away, got work at a convent — but I hated it. They were all so pious, but not one of those nuns had an ounce of love in her.'

'So what made you come West?' he asked.

'I was just fifteen when I learned about these catalogues, where you could have your name listed — and if you were lucky some fellow wanting a wife would contact you. That's how I heard from Seamus.'

He nodded, not wishing to push her if she felt she had told him enough. She continued unprompted.

'He met me off the train at Denver. Didn't recognize me at first because I was so young. He'd been expecting a much more mature woman, not somebody, as he put it, who'd just stepped out of the cradle. I guess I'd misled him about my age. In my letters, I gave the impression I was middle aged. He said he couldn't possibly marry me till I was grown up.'

Rice shook his head in disbelief. 'So what happened?'

'Well, Seamus gave me the money for my return rail fare, but there wasn't a train running till next day so he took me to his house and made up a bed in his spare room. Next morning I cooked his breakfast and he really enjoyed it, so much so he eventually said I could stay on, be his housekeeper as a temporary measure, until I was old enough for marriage. Rice, he was so kind to me, I figured I was the luckiest girl in the world.'

'So when did you marry?'

She smiled reflectively. 'Never actually married. He said we might when we moved to Bull Crossing — but it never seemed appropriate somehow.'

He was astonished, lost for words.

'But one thing's certain,' she went on. 'I can never desert him. He made my life worth living and he needs me to make certain he's sober when he needs to be. I love him, you see.'

Sudden hope had flared in Rice, but it had been dashed.

'Sure,' he said sadly. 'I understand.'

★ ★ ★

A week later, when Able Early crossed Travis Mountain on his way to visit

Rice, he rode warily, forever conscious that Vince Corby would some day come hunting for him. He kept his Remington, loaded and ready, across the saddle in front of him, his eyes scanning both sides of the trail. He reached the point where Seth and Rice had been bushwhacked, gazed with sombre eyes at the cedar tree from which his brother had been lynched, and the grief that cut through him, sharp as a knife, started him coughing. When he recovered he rode on.

He was anxious to see how Rice was convalescing because, being short-handed at the Double Star, he needed the young cowboy back to work as soon as possible. He also needed the reassurance of having another gun around.

When he splashed across the ford into Bull Crossing and was riding up the street towards Doc Finnegan's, he took satisfaction in the belief that his journey had been unobserved, that Corby must be still far to the south. Even so, he went cautiously, keeping a watchful eye open for Thomas McAllister. The last thing he wanted was a confrontation with the tight-fisted Scotsman.

A half-hour earlier, when Able had passed beneath an overhanging rock, he could have been shot by the man observing him from just a few feet above. It would have been as easy as shooting a cow in a pen. Teevis had hugged himself low on the sun-warmed rock like a watchful, tail-twitching cougar. He'd fingered his rifle and remembered Vince Corby's words: *Find out if Able Early's still around. If he is, come back to me hell for leather. Don't let Early see you, don't harm him. That's a pleasure I'm savin' for myself. Understand?*

So Billy Teevis had let the rancher pass. Sure enough he'd tell Vince that the younger Early was still alive and that if he wished to introduce him to a rope's end, same as the older brother, that was his business. But Teevis hadn't given up on the other matter — the lust for vengeance which had drawn him and Charlie Rawlins to Bull Crossing. Teevis shuddered. The thought of Charlie's eyes, bulging with shock, as he'd pivoted around with the surgeon's knife jutting from his chest, had haunted him ever since, had caused him to twist fitfully in his blanket at night. Those disastrous minutes at the doctor's house had scared the wits out of him, what with that she-cat on his back and the surgeon reaching for a second knife. But after the initial panic, after he'd found refuge in the mountains above the town, he'd taken stock, figured he wasn't ready to return to Corby just yet.

Now, he mentally listed his grievances: the humiliation before the stampede; the fact that half his ear had been shot away and was paining him so bad it sometimes made him dizzy; the fact that by now, Charlie Rawlins' body would have been spaded into an unmarked grave in the bone-orchard on the edge of Bull Crossing. Over the past days, Teevis had kept watch on the town and on the trails which led in and out. He'd seen the surgeon ride away, his black medical bag across his saddle, no doubt containing his instruments. Teevis wondered if Charlie's blood had been wiped from that damned knife.

He'd spent hours on the hill directly overlooking the main street, focusing the eye-glass he'd inherited from Rawlins on the doctor's place. He'd seen Rice Sheridan pacing up and down on the shaded porch, exercising his leg, the girl fussing over him, and he'd felt his blood pounding, his breath quickening.

And on two nights, with the moon concealed behind cloud, he'd drifted into town, unseen, spying on the doctor's house from the scrub land at the back, his rifle ready loaded, praying that Sheridan would show himself at a window — but he hadn't.

Teevis's feelings had gone far beyond a simple grudge. Hatred burned inside him like acid, hatred for Rice Sheridan whom he held responsible for all his troubles.

His yellow teeth chomped on a cud of baccy, then he spat and swore for the hundredth time that the kid would be dead long before he'd recovered from the surgeon's knife. With no doubt Corby impatient for news of Able Early, Teevis figured he could no longer wait for the young cowboy to offer himself as a target. He would have to go in and get him — and soon.

12

Able sat with Rice, occasionally coughing and using his handkerchief to wipe his lips. He explained how he had men out, combing the thickets for any cows that had previously been missed — and how scarce the pickings were. 'What we have got, we'll drive to the railhead in the fall.' He leaned forward, rested his thin hand on Rice's shoulder. 'I'm goin' to need you back real soon. I want you workin' with Brad as assistant foreman.'

Rice nodded, the prospect appealing to him.

'How much longer before that leg heals?' Able enquired.

'Finnegan says another few days and I can be back in the saddle. The whole wound has healed real fine. I guess I owe it to Magdalen as much as anybody.'

'Magdalen?' Able said, puzzled.

'Maggie,' Rice clarified. 'Every night she rests her hands on my leg, just lightly. I've never known anythin' like it. A wonderful warmth spreads upwards. I can feel the leg healin'.'

Able coughed, then added, showing no disbelief, 'I guess women have special powers, Rice. I've learned that for myself.'

For a moment Rice didn't speak; he was so wrapped up with thoughts of Maggie, but then he cottoned on to what Able had said and he asked, 'How?'

'Well, I was mighty low after Seth was killed. The cattle being rustled was like salt being rubbed into the wound. I figured I didn't have much to live for. God knows what I'd have done had not help arrived.'

'Help?'

'Sure. Seth's intended bride Gabriella Devaney and her brother Joshua turned up at the ranch. They've been downright astoundin' — miracle workers if you ask me . . . '

Rice was frowning. 'You mean they're still with you?'

'Sure they are. Moved in. They've both worked real hard, cleanin' everythin' up, turnin' it to a real home again. Gabriella's the best, truly sweetest female I've ever known. She's . . . '

'Jesus!' Rice gasped. 'She's a downright trickster; so is her brother. The only reason they came West was to swindle the money out of a wealthy rancher. Now your brother's dead, they've fixed their attentions on you, Able. They're after your money, nothin' else!'

Able laughed scornfully. 'What money? I'm nigh broke after losin' that herd — and losin' out to McAllister at poker.'

'But do they know that? Have you told her?'

Able shook his head. 'You're misjudgin' them, Rice. Gabriella told me about your unfortunate experience with her. How she thought you was Seth and . . . ' He chuckled to himself. 'She's awful sorry about that. Says she was too hard on you. It was a genuine misunderstandin'. She asked me to tell you that neither Joshua nor herself hold any grievance for what happened.'

Rice snorted his disgust. He was certain that Seth would soon have realized what Gabriella really wanted and sent her packing — but Able was being downright gullible.

'In fact,' Able continued, 'she and Joshua asked me to deliver this gift from them.' He reached into his pocket, took out a small smartly bound book. He handed it to Rice. It was a Bible.

'There's a dedication in it,' Able said.

Rice turned the first page, saw the neatly inscribed message. He read aloud slowly, which was the way he'd learned.

Prepare your heart to receive the love of the Lord and live by it. The righteous shall prosper, but

the candle of the wicked shall be
put out.

For Rice Sheridan from Joshua
and Gabriella Devaney.

Rice swallowed hard. He'd never had
a Bible before. For a moment he
wavered, then he said, 'It's just another
trick of theirs.'

'You'll see,' Able murmured. He
dragged out his watch from his vest
pocket. 'Guess it's time I got back.
Gabriella's been preparin' a special
meal for this evenin', just for a treat.
I tell you, Rice, she's a real angel. And
her brother . . . he don't say much, but
he's a good worker.'

Rice was not convinced. He wondered
if they were really sister and brother.
More likely they were just a couple
of tricksters bound together by the
common aim to swindle other folks
out of their money.

No matter what they were, he knew
nothing he could say would alter Able's
opinion of them.

On the evening after Able had departed, another visitor arrived at the Finnegan house, Jake Fenwick, who owned a small ranch on the land adjacent to the White River. He was breathless and harassed. His wife had gone into labour, things were not going well — could the doctor come directly? Finnegan nodded his agreement, filled his medical bag with the necessities, gave Maggie a farewell kiss on the cheek and rode out with the worried rancher. Dusk was creeping in; it was doubtful he would be back before the next day.

Later that night, Maggie heard the marshal's dog barking and wondered what disturbed it. Her thoughts slipped to the weasel-face man who had tried to kill Rice. She shivered and wondered if he was prowling somewhere out there in the darkness. When she mentioned her fears to Rice, he took his gunbelt from the dresser in the main room, checked the weapon and kept it close thereafter.

Beaulah Allchurch had prepared Harry's favourite supper — pork and boiled corn. When he'd got home from work, it awaited him on the table. Today was their eighth wedding anniversary and Beaulah's second marriage, her first husband having succumbed to a heart ailment. Her son by that earlier partnership was now eighteen and attending West Point Academy as an officer cadet. Beaulah was the daughter of a Washington rabbi, and she had not been born to the harshness of the West, but she had met Harry when he had visited Washington, had been fascinated by his fine nose which was bigger even than those of her Jewish friends. She had also been fascinated by the tales he told her of his experiences as a peace officer. Within a week she had agreed to marriage.

Beaulah was no wilting lily. She vigorously ran the Townswomen's Guild of Bull Crossing, which boasted four lady members, and did not include the half-dozen fallen doves of the saloon whom Beaulah considered a disgrace to their sex. Nor did it include the doctor's wife, young Maggie, who always kept to herself.

Harry loved Beaulah, despite her primness, and strove hard to maintain her standards of respectability. That was why, when supper was over and he sat smoking on his porch, the white dog curled at his feet, he couldn't help but pray that his past would stay where it belonged — dead and buried. However his brain kept worrying at it until there, in the gloaming of evening, when he should have been at peace, he was not, because the fearsome events of sixteen years ago rose in his mind as vividly as if they were on a stage in front of him — a stage where he, Harry Allchurch, was a leading player.

13

Way back in those days, old John
Early was still alive and striving hard
to establish his ranch, keeping the
Indians at bay. He had been irked
by the homesteaders who claimed
land under the 1862 Act, building
their soddies, planting their crops near
the best watering points. Frequently
they irrigated the streams, blocking
the water from flowing on to land
where he grazed his cows. One by
one, by fair means or foul, he drove
them away, made life so downright
miserable for them that they gave up
— that is all except one family, the
Sheridans who had staked their claim
in the valley close to the head of the
Fresno Canyon.

At that time, before he sought to
hide his past behind an image of
respectability, big-nosed Harry Allchurch

worked for the Earlys as a hired hand. He and the Early boys were wild spirits, hoorawing into Bull Crossing, shooting up the town more than once, going on drunken sprees, young Able trying to keep pace despite his lungs.

They hadn't much time for the homesteaders normally, but that spring Seth took to spying out on the Sheridan place, just to get sight of the woman. She had a small kid and her husband was away an awful lot, mixing with local riff-raff. Harry understood why Seth was so stricken, because he shared the same lusts. Females hadn't yet arrived at Bull Crossing and a man got awful horny just thinking about what he was missing. That was why Laurina Sheridan had no right to flaunt herself the way she did, hanging unmentionable garments on her clothes line, swinging her hips and giving her coy, meaningful looks to all and sundry. Mind you, she was a fine-looking woman, with a full body that she did little to conceal. Seth said it made him stiffen up, just laying his eyes on her. Able would snigger, and Harry wouldn't say much because he knew damned well he hungered after Laurina just as bad as the Earlys.

Maybe John Early was aware of the disturbing influence this woman had on his sons — maybe that was another reason he wanted the Sheridans gone from his land. He abhorred fiercely any lustful thoughts or sins of the flesh in his sons.

On the morning when it all happened, he was in no mood for further negotiation with the homesteaders. He had warned the Sheridans that unless they cleared out voluntarily, he would expel them by force. At that time, the only law in the territory was a man's conscience. And, despite his religious ideas, John Early did not consider that the strict rules of the Bible were intended to stop him from expelling squatters and sodbusters.

So he sent Seth, Able and Harry to deliver a final message. It was unfortunate that they took the long, circuitous route to the homestead painting their tonsils in the saloon at Bull Crossing. Afterwards, as they rode meanderingly across the range, supping whiskey as they went, Seth spotted dust in the far distance. They pulled up and presently saw a line of Indian riders, the whiteness of their feathers catching the sun — Kiowa. The sight of the Indians, disappearing into the distance, sobered them. Kiowa were not healthy to have around, not since old Sitting Bear had started boasting that he would exterminate all the whites in Texas.

Soon they pushed on, their spirits rising again. When they topped that last ridge and gazed down at the wretched soddy, they were liquored up to their ears. The sight of the woman, soaping washing in a tub just outside the door, the kid, a younker, making mud-pies in the dust at her feet, had them tittering and mouthing lewd comments.

Hearing them, Laurina raised her head, her glance half-frightened, half defiant. She took the child's hand, led him back inside.

'Seems her man's away,' Able said.

'She must be lonely,' Seth grinned. 'Maybe we should give her a li'l company.'

Harry had nodded, feeling his sap rising.

But they were wrong about her being alone. As they pushed down into the valley and approached the soddy, Sheridan himself appeared in the doorway, hoisting up his galluses, a rifle in his hand. He was a big man and his threatening stance made all three visitors momentarily forget the woman.

Seth yelled, 'Pa says you gotta get off this land!'

'We claimed it fair and square under the Homestead Act,' Sheridan shouted. 'We got rights here. Now ride the hell outa here or I'll fill you with lead!'

'We got more rights than you, mister,' Seth rejoined and he slipped his own rifle from his scabbard. 'We

144

got three guns to your one.'

With cool deliberation, Sheridan raised his rifle to his shoulder, took aim and fired. Whether or not he intended to hit anybody was never clear, but the bullet whined so angry close to Seth that he reacted by pulling his own trigger. The slug mangled high into Sheridan's chest, bloodying his shirt, sending him tumbling backwards into the soddy. Through the doorway, they saw that the woman was suddenly stooping over him, screaming out in anguish, then she quieted, stared straight at them, her coy looks long gone. She called them names so foul that a woman should never have known them.

Stung by her abuse, Seth said, 'Let's go teach that bitch a lesson!' And all three slid from their horses, and moved down towards the soddy, their pace quickening. The woman had dragged her husband's body back inside, temporarily disappearing. Harry was first through the door, stumbling over the body, whiskey making his vision red. The woman was backed against the far wall, her eyes wide with terror, her breasts heaving.

'She's asked for this!' Seth yelled, unbuttoning his britches. 'My God, she's kept me waitin' long enough!' The others did likewise and shortly Laurina's dress had been ripped back, exposing her white breasts, and she went down, her screams growing shrill as she struggled in vain, her body jerking desperately as she was penetrated again, and again, and again . . .

Harry always figured he was the first to regain his sanity — first to notice how the woman's screaming had ceased, how Seth's hands were somehow wrapped around her throat. She'd stopped writhing and had gone awful still; her feverish eyes had turned glassy. 'Oh God, she's dead!' Harry cried out.

It was then they started to tremble and to ask themselves why they had done this hideous thing.

All three were sated, exhausted — and for a time the only sound was the pant of their breathing, but this gradually steadied and a cough erupted from Able's narrow chest, then in a husky voice he asked, 'What will Pa do when he finds out?'

Seth tried to speak but somehow couldn't, so it was Harry who made the suggestion, 'Let's burn the place to ashes. Let's say the Injuns did it.'

Seth and Able exchanged glances, then they nodded.

They found some kerosene in the back room, doused the furniture and walls. Harry even climbed up, sprinkled kerosene across the timbers and sod of the roof. As he worked, the sky had gone almost black and thunder rumbled out, scaring the wits out of him. Afterwards he swore it was God's wrath.

With everything ready, they lit torches, tossed them on to the roof, the flames seizing hold with a crackle.

They mounted their horses and Able

asked, 'What happened to the kid?'

Seth looked around, uncertainty branded across his face. 'God knows!' he said. It was too late now to re-enter the burning abode. So they kicked their animals into motion and fled from that valley, the awesomeness of what they'd done reflecting in their tight-lipped silence. And as they raced on, the heavens split open. Large spots of rain pelted down, driving into them and their horses like hard pebbles. The elements flashed and roared with such fury that they cowered in their saddles, their souls scarred, their lives changed for always.

14

Dusk was misting the land as Able Early returned to the Double Star following his visit to the recovering Rice — and the ride across Travis Mountain had taken its toll. He was weary, had difficulty getting his breath and there was blood across the back of his hand when he coughed. He put his horse to pasture and was walking towards the house when he saw Joshua Devaney washing at the kitchen water-pump. The big man was something of a puzzlement for he seldom spoke or smiled. He spent hours sitting on the porch, studying his Bible, sometimes whispering as if reading aloud, though once as Able stepped close he imagined he heard cuss-words rather than holy words. Now Joshua gave Able a nod and said, 'Mister Early, you've got a visitor up at the house.'

A minute later Able found Major Ed Buckley sitting in the main room, smoking his pipe and drinking the coffee Gabriella had brought him. Buckley owned a neighbouring ranch and he'd been a participant in that poker game when Able had lost out heavily to the Scotsman Thomas McAllister.

Gabriella, looking attractive and ebullient, had been charming the visiting rancher as he waited for Able's return. Now he was here, she poured another coffee and left them to their business.

Buckley was a tall, angular man with tufty sideburns and a doleful expression, but Gabriella had put a twinkle in his eye, and he remarked, 'You sure are lucky, Able, havin' a housekeeper like that lady.'

Able nodded. 'I figure she was sent from heaven.'

Buckley's mood now changed. He glanced furtively around as if to make sure they were not overheard. It was clear he had serious business on his mind, business that was troubling him. 'Ever since you lost out to Thomas McAllister,' he said, 'I been unable to sleep at night.'

Able coughed and said nothing. He'd always looked upon Buckley as a rival, whether in cards or cattle, never trusted him any more than he did the Scotsman. He figured he might have misjudged him.

'Able, I can't let things rest. I discussed it with my wife. She said I should speak to you. The fact is I can't let McAllister cheat you. It just ain't Christian.'

'What're you gettin' at?'

'What I'm sayin' is he was usin' trimmed cards playin' both ends against the middle.'

Excitement brought a quiver to Able's nostrils. 'How do you know?'

'He's always had a reputation as a card-sharp, belonged to a poker ring in Denver before he came here. I checked the cards when he was mouthin' off to you that night. I even kept one. It was trimmed neat as a whistle! Look, I got it here.' He reached into his coat pocket, drew it out and slipped it across the table to Able. 'Run your finger down the left side. You'll feel it's uneven.'

Able complied, nodded.

Buckley went on, 'Haven't you noticed the way he always wears gloves, pampers his hands, keeps them sensitive to every shavin' in the cards?'

'Sweet Jesus!' Able exhaled in amazement. 'Well, I'll be . . . ' Then his eyes narrowed as the implication of Buckley's words sank home. 'Are you sayin' that if McAllister pushes his claim, you'll testify for me?'

Buckley sat turning his cup around in his rough hands, steeling himself for a hard decision, then he said, 'Sure I will. But maybe it won't come to that. Maybe I can head him off.'

Able suddenly felt light-headed with joy. Sure, his prize critters were lost — but at least what was left would still be his. He reached over the table, shook the other man's hand. 'I'm real beholden to you,' he said, 'real beholden.'

As Buckley rose, he said, 'You ain't lookin' too well, Able. You best take care of yourself, otherwise you'll end up buried alongside your brother.'

Able nodded. A short while back he had welcomed such a prospect. Now everything was changing. 'What you've told me, Ed, has perked me up no end. I ain't ready for the grave yet.'

★ ★ ★

It was an hour later when Gabriella took Able's thin hand in hers and said, 'Able, honey, you feel so cold. I'm really worried about you. Maybe you should have an early night. I'll bring supper to you.'

Able gazed at her, still unable to believe his luck at having such a considerate and beautiful woman to care for him. The sight of her womanly body, the heady smell of the scent she wore, stirred old lusts in him, lusts that he had stifled since the death of Laurina Sheridan sixteen years since. From then on, he'd not touched another woman, the mere thought filling him with disgust at himself. Now, as a man, he was too physically sick to satisfy a woman or consider marriage, particularly to a female so vibrant, so full of life as Gabriella — yet she treated him with more respect than he'd thought possible. She made him feel he had qualities which he, and everybody else, had overlooked.

'Gabriella,' he murmured, finding himself lost in her blue eyes, 'I'm truly grateful to you and Joshua for movin' in. I hope you'll stay permanent.'

'We'll stay here as long as you want us, Able. That's the least we can do after all you've suffered. Well . . . ' she hesitated, 'that's speaking for myself. Joshua would like to stay till he can launch his ambitions.'

'Ambitions?'

She nodded. 'Joshua came West with me because he believed there was work to be done out here. When he discovered that Bull Crossing had no church, he saw the desperate need of local folks, the desperate need for the Lord. I guess you could say he's preparing himself for a sort of ministry. His aim is to save as many souls and as many sinners as he can.'

'I see,' Able murmured, figuring he now understood Joshua better. 'There's an ample supply of sinners around here,' he murmured.

He was conscious of Gabriella's eyes gazing at him. Seeing her in the lamp-glow, he fancied he saw sadness in those eyes. He suddenly felt ashamed, wondering if she could see what was in his head, see the awful guilt that had been there for sixteen years.

When he was in his bed, his thoughts drifted backwards as they so often did, despite his efforts to turn his mind to more agreeable things. He recalled how, after wiping out the Sheridan homestead, Seth, himself and big-nosed Harry Allchurch had returned to the ranch and over the next few days busied themselves with work, keeping their heads down, praying that John Early would never find out what had happened.

On the fourth day, Allchurch expressed concern that the rain could have doused the fire they'd started, leaving the soddy standing with its grisly evidence for all to see. So the three of them rode out to that awesome valley, now dried out by the sun. Sure enough the scorched soddy still stood. They couldn't face going inside, seeing the bodies again, so they retorched it from the outside, this time making sure that afterwards only ashes remained. Later, they helped spread rumours of Indian pillage and were relieved when this version of events was accepted. The fact was that folks would believe anything bad about the Indians, they were that riled up with hatred.

But whilst the Indians were blamed

for the Sheridan massacre and the incident gradually faded into history, the shame of the three men didn't. Their personalities changed. Seth turned to religion, — spending long hours on his knees, begging the Lord for forgiveness. Able's lung sickness and mental torment drew him deeper and deeper into wretchedness. Harry Allchurch left the Earlys, swore himself to temperance, renounced profanity and in due course became town marshal at Bull Crossing; later he found himself a wife who seemed the pinnacle of respectability. And old John Early went to his grave, never knowing why his sons had given up their hoorawing ways.

When Seth had realized that the boy who came to the ranch seeking work was none other than the Sheridan child, he had seen it as a God-sent opportunity to redress his sins. He had treated Rice with great kindness, almost as his own son, the young cowboy never guessing the true motive.

Now, through the long night-hours, Able was restless, haunted by the past, coughing and ill. But somehow Gabriella and her compassion had given him the will to cling to life. And then there was Joshua — and his aim to save sinners. Able saw them as a truly noble couple intent on helping others.

He hoped that his brother Seth had found redemption up there beyond the Golden Gate, his fortunes swayed by the kindness he had shown to Rice Sheridan. Tonight Able sensed that he had been offered a chance to gain grace himself. His mind turned to the last will and testament he had completed after Seth's death. In this he had bequeathed all he owned to his only relative — a nephew living in the north, whom he had never met. He now made a decision; he had an opportunity to give some purpose to his life. He would leave the ranch and everything he possessed to those he considered more worthy than anybody else in the world — the Devaneys.

15

Maggie Finnegan shuddered as she heard the dog barking. Outside a cooling breeze had lifted into the darkness. She looked through the window of the parlour, out towards the scrub-land at the rear. She could see a faint glimmer of light from Marshal Allchurch's cabin, but otherwise everything was black. There was no moon. She turned back into the parlour. Rice was sitting at the table, cleaning his Colt. He looked up, smiled, and her heart gave a little leap.

Rice's leg was still sore, but he knew it would support him, that it was only a matter of time before he was fully fit. He owed a lot to Seamus Finnegan, Sabine — and the girl with the healing touch.

She now produced a board and some checkers and set them out on the low table. They sat, moving the pieces around, smiling, but their minds weren't really on the game, and shortly their hands touched. He looked at her. She laughed and he felt a sensation in his cheeks, and he couldn't tear his gaze away from her smiling pink lips. She moistened them with the tip of her tongue, making them glisten.

She said, 'I'm tired of playing checkers, Rice. Let's sit on the sofa. It'll be more comfortable for you.'

He nodded. He was desperate to take her in his arms, to kiss her — and she sensed his thoughts because as they settled onto the sofa, she said, 'You can if you like, Rice!' and she inclined her head, her hazel eyes misting to dreaminess.

'Magdalen' he murmured. 'I . . . ' The nearness of her made him swell, but his conscience troubled him. 'Magdalen . . . how about Seamus?'

She had drawn close, her black hair brushing his face. 'He's been like a father, a good father. That's all.' Then, almost matter of fact she added, 'Kiss me, Rice. I'll die if you don't.'

So he slipped his arm around her shoulders and the warm fullness of her body melted into him. Her lips were trembling. They opened like a moist flower under his and he had never tasted anything so sweet, so heavenly.

When at last she drew back, his senses were clamouring and he gasped, 'God . . . Magdalen . . . where d'you learn to kiss like that?'

'My Uncle Bob . . . that's why I had to run away, Rice.'

He regretted reminding her of unhappy memories. He said, 'Poor Magdalen . . . ' and kissed her again, and in that golden wonderful moment, she drew his hand to her blouse, guided his fingers to the buttons, groaning in ecstasy.

From outside, Allchurch's dog resumed its barking. This time it sounded closer and frenzied. Abruptly, the barking ceased. Silence flowed back, made more intense by the rapid breathing of Rice and Maggie.

Conscious that they were bathed in lantern glow and visible from outside, Rice rose to his feet, still tremulous from passion, but knowing that the moment had been destroyed.

'We'd best put the shutters across the windows,' Maggie whispered.

He limped to the door, opened it, peered into the darkness and saw nothing.

'Rice, have this!'

He glanced back. She was holding up his gun. He slipped it into his waistband. Together, they went out on to the back porch, found the heavy shutters and started to lift them against the window.

That was when the shot blasted off.

Wood splintered spitefully. Lead had clipped the porch support. Maggie cried out, fell back. Rice had also fallen, thinking he had been shot, but he moved his arms and legs and realized he was unscathed. He twisted and saw Maggie lying in the open doorway, blood darkening the side of her face. He cried out in alarm, but at that moment two more shots came in quick succession, the bullets thudding into the boards of the wall. Fury erupted in him. He snatched his Colt from his waistband, scrambled up and fired blindly into the darkness — all five shots in the chamber.

In the clamorous, ringing hush which followed, he stood, the blood pounding in his temples, his breath heaving, then he turned back and crouched over the girl, despair cutting through him. Thankfully, she was moving; her eyes opened and she stared up into his face.

'Magdalen . . . ' he gasped.

She touched her head, glanced at her bloody fingers and said, 'I'm all right. Splinters caught me, I guess.'

They both tensed as a voice called to them from out of the gloom. Rice straightened up. The voice came again. 'Don't shoot. It's me, Harry Allchurch!'

Rice went forward, favouring his leg, his eyes adjusting to the night. He saw how the marshal had come up from his cabin and, with his gun levelled, was gazing at something on the ground . . . a man's body. 'You sure did some fancy shootin', Rice Sheridan,' Allchurch proclaimed, 'but this feller ain't dead — yet.'

Rice reached them, aware that Maggie had followed him, was clinging to his arm. Other folks were approaching cautiously from the street, disturbed by the sound of shots.

'He knifed my dog,' Allchurch complained. 'Who is he?'

Rice peered down, saw the man's weasel-features, jutting teeth, heard the groan wheezing up from his innards and knew well enough who he was. He was dying, no doubt about that — even so, his eyes swivelled, settling on the young cowboy; his lips moved and the words came so husky-low they were scarcely audible. 'You got me, Sheridan, but Corby'll come back . . . Corby'll come back. He'll string up Able Early, same as he did his brother . . . then he'll kill you . . . '

Teevis convulsed, death rattling in his throat, then he expired, but his words lingered chillingly, like a curse, and all Rice could do was hug the sobbing Maggie and thank God the outlaw's aim hadn't been as deadly as his intent.

For the first time in his life, Rice Sheridan had killed a man. And for the second time in his life, he had kissed a woman.

16

'Sure I know them,' Harry Allchurch said as he studied the Wanted notice he had been handed, recognizing the man and woman depicted thereon. It was a week into the killing of the outlaw Billy Teevis and Bull Crossing had slumped back into its customary torpor — but this morning a stranger had ridden into town, quickly found the marshal's office and introduced himself. He was a heavy-jowled, dark man with a German accent. In the saddle he seemed tall, but on the ground he looked squat because his legs were stubby. Astride his horse or not, there was nothing insignificant about his demeanour. He was bull-tough. His name was Carl Schwartz and he was from the Pinkerton National Detective Agency in Chicago.

'Sure I know them,' Allchurch

repeated, brushing away a fly that was pestering his big nose. 'They're the couple who've moved in over at the Double Star. She's doin' housekeepin' for Able Early.'

Schwartz laughed scornfully. 'They are wanted in half-a-dozen states for robbery, extortion, fraud, bigamy . . . you name it, they have done it. Short of murder, folks do not come much blacker than these two. The woman specializes in posing as a mail-order bride. Always picks a wealthy victim, and . . . ' He rubbed his finger and thumb together expressively, then he patted his pocket. 'I have a warrant for their arrest. *Ja!* All I want now is to get the job done.'

'Like I say,' Allchurch nodded, 'you'll find 'em over at the Double Star Ranch. Always figured they was too good to be true.'

'Marshal,' the Pinkerton man said, 'I could do with some assistance in apprehending those two. Things are always tricky when a woman's involved.

Will you come with me?'

Allchurch shrugged. 'I hadn't figured on leavin' town today . . . but it'll be good to get those tricksters into custody. Sure I'll come. There's somebody else headin' that way too. Young Rice Sheridan works at the Double Star. He's just recovered from a leg wound. I guess he'll welcome the company.'

Schwartz nodded. He went across to the town's restaurant and had a breakfast, while Allchurch returned to his cabin and told Beaulah he would be late for supper, or maybe he would not be back that night. The marshal then visited Doc Finnegan's where he informed Rice that he'd have company when he rode to the ranch.

A half-hour later all three were on their way, Rice carrying a bottle of medicine for Able from Doc Finnegan. As they rode, the coolness of air at the higher levels was a welcome relief after the simmering heat of the town. Excitement showed in the detective's face. He had spent six tedious months searching for the tricksters; now it seemed his quarry was at hand. Rice too felt satisfaction because his suspicions of the Devaneys had been vindicated. He hoped that Schwartz's arrival would not prove too late, that the Devaneys had not already fled, having inflicted some crippling damage on Able and the Double Star.

* * *

Joshua Devaney had been uneasy for days. In the past, he had preferred working on the move and in that way dodging those who would curtail his activities. But Gabriella had insisted they put down roots, at least for a while. She had maintained that they were safe in this corner of Texas, that Pinkerton and his agents would not reach this far. The pickings, she'd said, would make it all worth while. Of course Seth Early's death had come as a shock, but she declared that time spent on the ailing Able would reap

169

a rich reward. All it required was patience.

But Joshua was sick of playing his pious act. Admittedly, there was nothing like claiming you were performing the Lord's work to elicit trust from gullible folk, particularly those with guilty consciences which was nigh everybody — but the fact was that Joshua had grown nervous. He'd taken to roaming the hills above the ranch, keeping his eyes on the trail from Bull Crossing. And so it was, on this very morning, a cloud of dust caught his attention. Through it he saw three riders approaching. He recognized Rice Sheridan and Marshal Allchurch but he couldn't be sure about the third rider, although there was something familiar about his upright stance in the saddle — the dogged, seemingly relentless way he pushed his horse. Joshua turned cold. The name of Pinkerton reared in his mind and with it the recollection of several previous hair's-breadth escapes, each one paring down his reserve of luck until he was convinced that another brush with law enforcers would spell disaster.

He now decided that if Gabriella wished to linger in this place, then it was her affair. As for himself, he was leaving — but first he needed a horse. Brad Silvers the ranch foreman had loaned him mounts previously, and there would be no reason to suppose that this time anything more was intended than the normal leisurely ride across the range. Accordingly, Joshua hastened back to the ranch. Most likely those riders would pull in at the house first, and initially his absence wouldn't arouse any suspicions.

He found Brad Silvers talking to one of the new ranch-hands near a corral, and asked for a horse, hoping that the anxiousness didn't show in his voice. The foreman obliged, seeming to attach no significance to the feverish way in which Joshua saddled up and got mounted. Minutes later the bogus religious man was heeling his sorrel forward, not pausing for farewells or to collect his possessions. His most vital item of equipment was nestled in his pocket — his derringer pistol.

★ ★ ★

You got me, Sheridan, but Corby'll come back . . . Corby'll come back. He'll string Able up, same as he did his brother . . . then he'll kill you . . .

As he rode, Rice kept pondering on Teevis's ugly threat. Despite his concerns about the mischief Gabriella and her brother might have caused, he knew that the real danger lay with the outlaw leader. The question was not if he would return, but when, and Rice sensed it would be sooner rather than later. And the Double Star with its ailing boss and depleted manpower would be in no position to defend itself. Rice wondered if Able was fully aware of the danger, fully aware of the gruesome fate Corby planned for him. In fact, even now, he wondered what they would find when they returned to the ranch. Would they already be too late?

As they descended from the low hills and sent their horses across the flat, skirting the corral fences, the windmill and blacksmith shop, he noted with relief that all appeared quiet and he spotted Brad Silvers working down by the water-pump, exchanged a wave with him, and concluded that nothing untoward had happened as yet.

Anxious to avoid the Devaneys slipping through his grasp, Schwartz asked Harry Allchurch to circle around the back of the house in case the tricksters tried to make a break for it. The marshal nodded and rode off to comply.

Minutes later, Rice followed the detective up on to the porch and into the house. Entering the big main room, they came face to face with a dismayed Gabriella Devaney who was dusting the furniture. Schwartz was not swayed by her beautiful looks and feminine wiles, showing no chivalry towards the opposite sex other than that afforded by the business end of a Colt .45.

'Why, you've made an awful mistake . . . ' she was complaining as with long-practised ease the detective pinned her against the wall, got handcuffs around her wrists and snapped them shut.

'Where's your partner-in-crime?' he demanded. 'It will do you no good to tell me lies!'

Gabriella attempted her innocent act, fluttering her eyelashes, but Schwartz burned her with such a malevolent glare, that she submitted, crumbling like a spent flower. 'He's gone,' she said. 'I doubt he'll come back.'

Schwartz cursed. Harry Allchurch had now come in. 'I just spoke to Brad Silvers,' he said. 'About fifteen minutes ago, Joshua Devaney borrowed a horse, rode out to the south.'

Rice said, 'Leave him to me. I'll find him, bring him back,' then he asked, 'Where's Able?'

Gabriella spoke out as if blaming them for Able's plight. 'He's bedded down. He's sick. What you're doing today'll probably kill him.'

Rice hesitated. He reached into his pocket, took out the medicine Finnegan had sent. 'Best give him this, Marshal.' He passed the bottle to Allchurch, then the thought that every minute's delay gave Joshua a better chance of escape goaded him into action. 'I'll be back just as soon as I can.'

A few minutes later, he was down at the meadow, saddling a fresh animal, a sturdy grulla, and ensuring that he had a good rope. He then rode away from the ranch, heading south. He had one important advantage over the fleeing trickster: he knew the country.

17

Able's lungs were wheezing as he struggled for breath. He was deathly pale as he lay in his bed, fixed for him in a downstairs room by Gabriella. A disbelieving light sparked in his face when Carl Schwartz revealed the purpose of his visit. From the next room came the sound of Gabriella's despairing sob. The detective had chained her to an empty gun-rack on the wall. Gradually her sobbing gave way to a steady stream of curse words, totally out of keeping with the gentle image she had previously adopted.

Able had been propped up on his pillow, his eyes dull and red-rimmed. He had been working, albeit with a weak and quivering hand, on his new will; now his pen had paused. 'I don't believe you,' he gasped.

The detective shrugged his shoulders.

'Whether you believe me or not, Mister Early, it does not make any difference to me. I have enough evidence to stand up in any court and ensure that Gabriella and Joshua Devaney end up where they belong — behind bars!'

'We've all been tricked,' Harry Allchurch cut in. 'It was lucky Carl Schwartz arrived when he did. The trouble is, we ain't caught Joshua yet.'

'I am relying on that young cowboy to bring him back,' the detective said. 'If he is not back by tomorrow morning, I will have to push on and at least get the woman to a jail.'

Able was gradually absorbing the truth, his tongue clicking in dismay. He was totally disillusioned. At last he emitted a long sigh of acceptance. He had no option. 'Rice'll bring Joshua back,' he said.

Gabriella's complaints from the next room were growing more demanding so the detective nodded to the ailing Able and stepped out.

Able struggled with a bout of

coughing. Harry Allchurch passed the medicine to him and he accepted it with relief, uncorking the bottle, slurping it back like whiskey. 'Sure glad I got that, Harry,' he murmured. 'It's the only thing that helps.'

Able gazed down at the paper before him. 'I suppose I must be grateful for not makin' a fool o' myself,' he grunted, then he sighed again. 'I don't think I've got long left in this world, Harry. Thinkin' back, I guess neither of us have much to be proud of, not regardin' what we did sixteen years ago.'

Allchurch cleared his throat nervously. This was not a subject he liked to discuss. 'Best to let sleepin' dogs lie, Able.'

'No,' Able said firmly. 'The truth is bound to come out one day. It's best that we make a clean breast of it now, that we confess. At least then we can go to our graves knowin' that we ain't hidin' anythin'.'

The marshal gazed at Able, horrified.

If any whisper of those bygone events crept out, he would be ruined — his family, his position, the respect he'd tried so hard to build. 'You can't do that, Able,' he said emphatically.

Able seemed not to hear him. 'I'm convinced it's the only way. I figured I could somehow make up for what we did by leavin' all I had to the Devaneys, them being so set on doing worthy work. Now that's no longer a choice, this is the only way.'

Anger flared in Allchurch. 'You can't do that, Able. If you let on, you'll drag us all down.' He rose to his feet so suddenly that he knocked the medicine bottle over, sent it dropping to the floor and heard the gurgle as the contents soaked into the boards.

Able didn't even comment. His thoughts were so focused on his words. 'My mind's made up. I'll die with a clear conscience. I'm going to confess, Harry.'

'You can't do that, Able!'

'I can, Harry . . . and I will.'

179

Angrily, Allchurch stamped from the room, aware that whatever else happened, he couldn't allow his whole future and livelihood to be jeopardized by this foolish man.

★ ★ ★

An hour after leaving the Double Star ranch, Rice found the sign he was seeking — the hoof-marks of a hard-pressed horse along the sandy banks of a small stream, but presently these disappeared as the ground became rocky. He surmised that Devaney would be making for the way-station at Kiowa Springs; the wild terrain offered little else in between. Thereafter he would probably aim to take a stage eastward towards Houston and maybe Louisiana. But Rice had no intention of allowing him to get that far.

Long familiar with the country, the young cowboy abandoned the trails as they twisted along the canyon bottoms; instead, he moved cross-country via higher ground, his intention being to get ahead of his quarry. In early afternoon he topped out on the western rim of the vast Eagle Canyon and gazed downward across terrain speckled with juniper and buttonbrush. In the base of the canyon a stream glinted in the sun.

He strained his eyes, desperately seeking some movement, trying to differentiate between the countless clumps of distant brush and the moving shape of man and horse. At last he spotted a sliver of dust but grunted in disappointment as he realized this was not raised by a single horseman. It came from three small wagons heading westward. He debated whether or not to ride down and enquire if the wagoners, probably whiskey-traders, had encountered the fleeing trickster and was about to do so when another movement caught his eye. Now his blood began to pound with excitement. A lone rider had been halted in a cottonwood clump, concealing himself as the wagons passed; now he was pressing on again.

Rice heeled his grulla forward, sensing that he must move quickly. Of course, the distant figure might not be Devaney, but he sensed that it was. He angled down the incline, ensuring his quarry was in sight, then, keeping to the treacherous slope he cut through taller sage and juniper, thankful that his animal was sure-footed. Within a half-hour he had established that his surmising had been correct. The horseman was indeed Joshua Devaney.

A further twenty minutes of hard-riding saw him ahead of the trickster, and now the canyon trail had narrowed down, rising steadily. Rice dismounted, tethered the grulla and concealed himself in some boulders. The unsuspecting Devaney passed so close he could have brought him down with a pistol shot, but instead he allowed him to pass before stepping from cover with his rope at the ready. Devaney twisted as he heard the swish of the lariat, but he was too late to prevent the loop dropping neatly over his shoulders and jerking tight. He was immediately yanked from his saddle, his body hitting the trail with a jarring thud.

Despite the fall, Devaney was groping for his derringer as Rice leaped upon him. The big Easterner got the gun out, striving to level it but Rice gripped his brawny arm. The gun went off, the bullet whizzing skyward, and then he forced Devaney's fingers to release the tiny weapon. He had now drawn his own Colt, his eyes wild. Fear showed in Devaney's face and he nodded in submission. 'Don't shoot. For God's sake don't shoot!'

Rice did not trust him one iota. He kept him covered as he circled around him, roping him securely until he was satisfied that there could be no escape.

Devaney's horse had galloped onward and Rice did not take the chance of chasing after it. Instead, he mounted his own horse and set out on the return journey with the sullen-faced trickster stumbling along at rope's end, his blaspheming far removed from his recent pious manner.

The young cowboy was satisfied with his day's work, but he sensed that the main threat was still to come. Even so he was utterly unprepared for the shock that was awaiting him back at the Double Star.

18

It was long after midnight when they topped the rise overlooking the ranchhouse. The journey had been slow, with the exhausted Devaney stumbling and falling on occasions, but Rice had shown little mercy, being anxious to hand his charge over to the Pinkerton man as soon as possible. Now, as he gazed down, the moonlit ranchhouse seemed deadly still. No lamps shone from the bunkhouse nor from the main abode. Cautiously Rice tugged Devaney forward and touched his heels to the flanks of the weary grulla.

As they got closer he could see that the windows of the house were heavily shuttered. They were moving across the open ground fronting the porch when the challenge came, 'Who's there?' The voice, calling from inside, was not familiar to Rice, and it was backed by the metallic sound of a gun being cocked.

'Rice Sheridan,' he called back, reining-in and waiting anxiously, conscious that sitting here in the moonlight, he was a perfect target.

To his relief a more friendly response now came. 'Come on in then!' He heard bolts being drawn back, then a creak as the main door was pulled open.

He slipped from his saddle and, leading Devaney like a reluctant hound, climbed on to the porch and entered the house.

The main room was lit by an oil lamp, its glow shielded from the outside by shutters. The faces of all those inside were anxious and pale. Harry Allchurch, Schwartz the Pinkerton man, Brad Silvers the foreman, Lo Sang the Chinese cook, a sullen-looking Gabriella fretting at being chained to the gun rack and three young ranch-hands taken into employ during Rice's absence. It was one of these who had challenged him a few minutes earlier. Apart from Gabriella, everybody was gripping a gun of some sort.

It was Joshua who was first to speak as they entered the room. He would have jerked free of the rope if Rice had slackened his grip, but the young cowboy hung on as fury erupted from his prisoner, fury directed at Gabriella. 'You lowdown bitch! I told you we shouldn't have stayed in this place. We should've moved out when we had the chance!'

'Don't you call me a bitch,' Gabriella responded, her voice raised to a shriek. 'You'd have grabbed your share of the spoils, no mistake. Maybe if you hadn't run off, we could've worked something out!'

Carl Schwartz shouted at them to stop bickering, slipping in a few German curse words for the benefit of those who couldn't speak the language. He was greatly relieved that Rice had apprehended the fleeing Joshua. The detective soon snapped handcuffs about his wrists and released him from the confining grip of the rope.

'I will pull out at first light,' Schwartz commented. 'I will go back to Bull Crossing, get these beauties aboard the stage to San Antonio. The sooner I hand them over to the authorities the better.'

'Why's everywhere so forted up?' Rice enquired.

Brad Silvers answered. 'Yesterday afternoon I was in Bull Crossin'. Fred Carrington, the bartender at the Spotted Buffalo, told me a fellow had been in town askin' after the marshal. From his description, I'm damned sure it was Corby, Carrington told him Harry was out of town, had gone over to the Double Star. I got back here as quick as I could. If Corby's loiterin' around, he's sure to pay us a visit right soon. We figured it was best to be prepared.'

Vince Corby . . . Rice felt his insides twitch. So he was back at last.

'How's Able?' he asked. 'We'll need

every gun we can muster.'

There was a sudden silence. All eyes were on Harry Allchurch. The marshal cleared his throat. 'The news ain't good,' he said. 'Able's dead.'

'Dead!' Rice felt stunned.

'He shot hisself,' Allchurch said, 'right in front of my eyes. Just held his gun against his head and blew out his brains. He'd been goin' on about havin' nothin' to live for, but I didn't figure he'd act so sudden.'

Dazed by the marshal's words, Rice moved across the room, went through the door to where Able had had his bed. A low lamp had been left burning. Blood was splattered across the wall. He paused before the blanket shrouded body, then he reached out and drew back the cover. The sight sickened him. Half of Able's head had been blasted off, what was left of the brains inside the skull was exposed, but the eyes and mouth were open wide reflecting horror. Rice groaned, a sense of overwhelming loss in him.

Both Earlys had gone now. They'd been the nearest thing to a family he'd had since he'd left the Comanches. He put his thumb against each of Able's eyelids, easing them down over the eyes, shielding them from the troubles of the world.

Harry Allchurch had come in behind him. 'There was nothing I could do, Rice,' he repeated in a hushed voice. 'He asked to have his gun at hand in case Corby came burstin' in. I feel real bad about it.'

'I guess he'd had enough sufferin',' Rice murmured.

'That's for sure.'

Rice replaced the blanket and they returned to the main room.

'I wonder what's gonna happen to the ranch,' Allchurch said, 'now that Able's gone?'

Brad Silvers responded. 'I reckon it'll all go to his nephew up north.'

Carl Schwartz had been fastening his saddlebag. 'Before Able Early died,' he said, 'he gave me a sealed envelope containing his will. He requested me to make certain it got to his lawyer in San Antonio. I will surely do that.'

Allchurch spoke up sharply, 'I can save you that trouble, Mister Schwartz. I'll be visitin' San Antonio myself. I'll deliver that will.'

Schwartz shook his head. 'No. It is a duty I must carry out personally. I promised Mister Early.'

Allchurch frowned, but after a moment he regained his composure. 'If you ask me,' he said, 'the best thing would be to pack this place up and go somewhere safe until Corby has gone. Ain't healthy here with him hangin' around.'

'We can't do that,' Silvers cut in. 'There's animals to care for. The sooner we can take on more men to guard the ranch the better.'

'I'll send word to the Texas Rangers,' Allchurch commented. 'I'm sure they'll be mighty grateful to get their hands on Corby and his ruffians.' He glanced at Schwartz. 'I'll come with you when you leave at dawn and telegraph the

Rangers soon as I get back to Bull Crossin'.'

Gabriella suddenly complained: 'I don't figure I'm being treated with the respect due a lady, keeping me tied up like this. A lady has special needs.'

Schwartz gave her a fierce look. 'But madame,' he said, 'you are not a lady! I will accompany you to the out-house, but the hand-cuff stays put.'

Brad Silvers and his ranch-hands eased back the shutters from the windows so they could keep watch for the remaining night, allowing Allchurch and Schwartz to snatch some sleep. Rice sat in a chair and he too tried to doze, but his thoughts kept rambling, kept returning to Magdalen and the warm feeling she gave him. Just before he'd left the doctor's place that morning, she'd come to him and told him how Finnegan had tried to release her from any obligation to care for him. 'You're a young woman, Maggie. It ain't fair that you should be tied

192

up to an old drunkard like me. You need a young fellow, somebody like Rice Sheridan.'

But the old loyalty in her had stood firm. 'I'll not desert you, Seamus. Somebody's got to keep you on the straight and narrow.'

Drowsiness was taking hold of Rice when he heard a voice whispering his name. He opened his eyes, realized it was Gabriella calling to him from her uncomfortable position chained to the gunrack. He stood up, moved across to her, wondering what mischief she had in mind.

'Rice Sheridan,' she said. 'There's something you should know. Able Early didn't shoot himself. Look. From here, I can see into Able's room. I saw everything that happened.'

'You're lyin',' Rice said.

She shook her head. 'I've got no reason to lie now.'

'Well, if Able didn't kill himself, who did?'

She moved her position, trying to

get more comfortable, then she said: 'Harry Allchurch did it, fixed it to seem like suicide.'

Rice gasped with shock. 'Why should he do that?'

'Wanted to shut him up for some reason or other, I guess. You better ask him.'

Rice glared at Gabriella. All beauty seemed to have left her. He wondered how he had ever been attracted to her. Now she was a lost, humiliated creature but there was clearly one old skill that she retained: to make mischief. Maybe she felt that by stirring up trouble for the marshal, she might in some way contrive her own escape.

* * *

Harry Allchurch was trying to rest in Able's old study. He'd wrapped himself in a blanket, but he was plagued by the Pinkerton man's guttural snore. Schwartz had bedded down on the hard floor. Even his snore seemed to have a heavy German accent. Maybe in a normal bed he wouldn't snore so bad.

Allchurch was looking forward to getting home to his own bed and the warm comfort that Beaulah provided. His thoughts turned to Able whose mind had been set on confessing his sins, of revealing all that had happened at the Sheridan soddy those sixteen years since. That was something Allchurch could not allow. But killing him had stretched his nerve. Now he was haunted by Able's shocked expression as the gun had been levelled. Allchurch had fired point-blank into his head. His skull had seemed to explode, splashing blood all around. It had been easy to drop the weapon on the floor, to run from the room shouting that Able had killed himself.

Allchurch consoled himself with the belief that Able wouldn't have survived for long anyway. Now, nobody need ever know what had really happened just as nobody would ever know about his part in the Sheridan massacre. With regard to this, one matter still irked Allchurch. Schwartz had spoken of the will that Able had completed before his death, and that the sick man had asked him to convey it to San Antonio and lodge it with the family's lawyer. Allchurch did not care who inherited the ranch and the Early money. Able's nephew was welcome to that. But there might well be other implications. In his last will and testament, Able might well have bared his soul regarding the Sheridan incident — and if that information was revealed, Allchurch would be totally discredited.

Now, the marshal gazed across at the sleeping Pinkerton man, seeing how his head was resting on his saddle-bags. Able's final document was strapped into those bags. Allchurch started to plan. By dawn he had made up his mind. He would go with Schwartz when he set out, with his prisoners, for Bull Crossing. His presence would be welcomed as an additional escort.

On the way, he would attempt to bribe the Pinkerton man into giving up the contents of his saddle-bag. If he refused . . . Harry Allchurch had been involved in two deaths, and had successfully shifted blame away from himself. He would do it again and claim that Vince Corby had ambushed them, that he himself had only just escaped with his life. As for the Devaneys, he'd release them. They'd be thankful enough to disappear without trace. If they had any sense they'd steer clear of the law for the rest of their days. If they didn't, nobody would believe any cock-eyed stories they had to tell.

19

Rice was awake long before dawn, taking over from one of the hired-hands at his look-out post in the window of a room on the upper storey. As light drifted in across the valley, he gazed around the rims. All appeared quiet, just as it had on a thousand other mornings. He wondered where Corby was now, and when he intended to play his hand, whether he'd be satisfied once he learned of Able's death — or whether his vengeful lust would not be quelled until the Double Star was put to the torch, levelled to the ground, along with those inside.

Many possibilities twisted inside Rice's head. What future was there for him here? What sort of boss would Able's nephew be? Perhaps he'd sell up, having no wish to become involved with the ranch and all its tragedies.

Then his thoughts swung back to Magdalen. She was occupying more and more of his thinking time now. He felt sure he would never feel the same way about any other woman. He promised himself that if he survived whatever Corby had in mind, he'd ask her to marry him. If he could somehow offer assurance as to Seamus Finnegan's future, she might yet be swayed.

His musings were interrupted by the sound of movement from downstairs. He realized that Schwartz was getting ready to move his captives out.

So much had happened since Rice had set forth with Seth for the wedding in Bull Crossing, so much of it seemed unbelievable. He'd been plunged into a nightmare world which had stretched him to the extreme — and he had the harrowing feeling that the worst was yet to come.

★ ★ ★

Schwartz borrowed a buckboard wagon, provided by Brad Silvers, for the trip to Bull Crossing. In this were the Devaneys, securely handcuffed and bound, forced to sit alongside each other. This was much to their distaste for they exchanged hateful looks and constantly bickered, their language colourful, concerning the blame for their predicament. Schwartz carefully ensured that there would be no opportunity for them to escape, grunting with satisfaction as he made a final check of their bonds. He'd gratefully accepted Harry Allchurch's offer to escort him, and the party left the Double Star shortly after seven o'clock that morning, having eaten the breakfast provided by the Chinese cook with varying degrees of appetite. The marshal rode behind the wagon, his rifle slanted across his saddle, ostensibly keeping an eye on the surrounding terrain for sign of trouble.

The truth was that Allchurch was as anxious as anybody else to avoid the marauding Vince Corby and his ruffians, though he was mostly concerned with the contents of the Pinkerton man's saddle-bag — which Schwartz kept at his side as he sat on the wagon seat, his mount hitched to the rear. Allchurch had spoken of bringing in the Rangers to destroy Corby, but he had no intention of doing so. He'd pass a message to the undertaker that his services were required. If Corby was intent on inflicting vengeance on the Double Star, then let him do it. If Rice Sheridan perished in the process, then another segment of the past's damning jigsaw would have been destroyed.

It was an hour later when Schwartz had halted the wagon alongside a stream so that the horses could drink and allowed his prisoners a brief stretch of their limbs, that the marshal played his hand. He was determined to avoid bloodshed if he could, though that depended on the Pinkerton man's attitude.

'Mister Schwartz, I'd like to make you a proposal.'

Schwartz had just returned the sullen Devaneys to the wagon, making sure they were secure. He twisted round, cocked his head, waiting for Allchurch's next words.

'I'm interested in that document Able Early gave you — his will.'

'Ja,' Schwartz nodded. 'I will deliver it to the lawyer in San Antonio. I promised to do that.'

'That's just the point,' Allchurch persisted. 'For certain reasons I don't want that will delivered. I'm prepared to pay you well if you'll hand it over and forget you ever had it. I mean I'll pay you really well.'

Astonishment showed in Schwartz's heavy-jowled face. 'I promised a man who is now dead,' he said stubbornly. 'I will not break that promise!'

His statement was as solid as rock. It hung in the air between the two men, utterly impregnable. Allchurch knew that he had no option. 'OK,

Mister Schwartz. I see there's no changing your mind.' He feigned indifference, shrugging his shoulders, giving Schwartz time to move towards the wagon. Then, with the detective's back turned, he slipped his Colt from its holster.

Gabriella, sensing that she might be in the path of bullets, cried out in alarm. Schwartz, his reactions habitually razor-sharp, hurled himself to the side as the marshal's gun blazed off, his own weapon clearing leather. He fired through the haze of smoke created by the first shot, saw Allchurch recoil from sudden impact, stagger back and then collapse. The detective stepped forward, stood over the marshal's body, seeing how blood was spreading across his shirt-front — and knew that his bullet had killed. It had been a better shot than he'd intended. He recharged the empty cylinder in his gun and slipped the weapon back into his holster. He couldn't understand what had motivated Allchurch to behave so violently. He stepped over to the wagon, watched by the shocked Devaneys.

'Madame,' he said to Gabriella, 'you saved my life. For that I am grateful. The undertaker at Bull Crossing will be a busy man today.'

'Could you not show your gratitude by letting us go?' Gabriella pleaded.

Schwartz gave her a wistful smile, then he shook his head, climbed on to the wagon seat and rein-whipped the horse forward.

★ ★ ★

The gunfire had not gone unheard. Four riders had reined in on a higher slope, puzzled by the sound of shots coming from down through the trees. The tall, black-bearded man leading them said, 'Let's go see what's happenin' down there.' But as they urged their mounts forward, they heard the rattling progress of a wagon being driven at speed; far beneath them on the trail to town, the buckboard appeared.

'Who's them folk, Vince?'

Corby shook his head. He waited until the wagon had passed from view. He had no interest in the three occupants. He beckoned his men forward and shortly they discovered the body lying by the stream. Corby dismounted, hooked the corpse face-up with his booted toe. He grunted with surprise. 'Big-nosed Harry Allchurch,' he murmured, 'dead as a can of corned beef.'

He stepped back from the body and remounted his horse. 'Let's get to the Double Star and finish the job off.'

20

'He's here!' Brad Silvers had rushed back to the house from the corral, his voice sibilant, his face taut with alarm. 'I sure wish we had more men to defend this place.'

Rice nodded, checked his hand-gun and took up the rifle he had loaded and ready. Both men moved to the open window, gazing outward across the corral fences towards the hill slope to the south. Sure enough there were some ten riders approaching, looking like black buzzards against the lighter colour of the rising dust. 'Vince Corby damn him!' Silvers confirmed. 'Comin' back like we always knew he would.'

'Get the door bolted,' Rice shouted at the three hired hands, Blevins, Grant and Miller. All were youngsters no older than himself. They complied, but their faces were grudging. This wasn't their conflict; they had no wish to be here. But they were on the pay-roll and he guessed they'd fight if they had to.

Rice recalled the days when the ranch had been bustling with activity, the bunkhouse full of hired hands. Now everything had narrowed right down, with trail boss Will Carver and what remained of his men out on the far-flung lines and too few here to resist any attack.

But inside the room there was feverish activity. Lo Sang the Chinese cook had armed himself with a rifle. Brad Silvers would fight to the death if necessary, displaying blind loyalty. As for Rice, he knew that all their lives were at stake, that Corby would be desperate to complete the task he'd so nearly accomplished before. Rice was scared of the big outlaw; but hatred for him gave his fear a stubborn edge — a desire to do what was right by Seth and Able Early. Once again he reminded himself that this evil man Corby was responsible for all the tragedy that had befallen the Double Star. In a way Corby had killed Able as surely as he had Seth. Had it not been for the havoc he'd brought, life at the ranch would have gone on as normal. Now, it seemed that more men would die for a cause that was already lost.

Brad Silvers ordered the three hired hands on to the first floor, to keep watch back and front. Rice eased himself down behind an open window, slid the short double-tubed barrel of his Winchester across the sill. He saw how the sky was losing its starkness, the sun moving into its westward drift. He figured if they could hold out long enough, Harry Allchurch might be able to fetch in the Texas Rangers.

For maybe an hour they crouched and waited, the night taking hold, the silence in the valley only broken by the distant murmur of voices, sometimes laughter, that indicated that the outlaws were out there, obscured from view by the darkness and the shadowy block of the outhouses.

'They're bidin' their time,' Silvers muttered grimly. 'They know we'll damn well keep.'

'How long do you figure it'll take the Rangers to get here?' Rice asked.

'Well, if Allchurch telegraphed Fort Wallace soon as he got to town, I figure they should have been here by now, that's if they wanted to catch Corby.'

'Maybe if Corby was headin' back from town,' Rice muttered, half to himself, 'he bushwhacked the wagon.'

'I pray to God he didn't,' the foreman responded. 'If he did, we're in bad trouble. I guess . . . '

His words were interrupted by a voice calling to them, a deep, ominous voice coming out of the darkness that Rice immediately recognized as Corby's. 'I want Able Early. I've got you surrounded. If Able'll come out we can settle old scores and there'll be no more trouble.'

'Like hell there won't!' Silvers grunted. 'What're we gonna do, Rice?'

'Tell him Able's dead.'

Silvers nodded, cupped his hands to his mouth and yelled out, 'Able's dead. Shot hisself. His body's in here.'

There was a moment's stunned silence, then Corby called again. 'That's the fanciest story I ever heard. If he's dead, you just bring his body out here. That's the proof I'll need.'

'Damn him!' Silvers muttered. He looked at Rice, then he said, 'I worked for Seth and Able Early for six good years. They were mighty fine bosses, none better. I guess I'm not gonna give Able's body up to that devil. I'll see it's buried in the Christian way Able deserves.'

'Then I'll give Corby an answer he'll understand,' Rice grunted, and he lifted the Winchester into his shoulder, aimed out into the darkness towards where the outlaw's voice had come from and pressed the trigger.

The result was predictable. A fusillade of retaliatory shots hammered against the outer walls; upstairs, a window was shattered; a bullet whined through the open window close to Rice, thudded into the dresser, causing crockery to cascade down with a clatter.

The blast of shots subsided and then flames suddenly rose skyward. 'They're setting the bunkhouse alight,' Silvers stated. 'Thank God, there ain't no boys in there!'

Rice nodded. He suspected that when Corby had finished torching the outhouses, he'd turn his attention to the main house. Further shots shook the walls, causing them to duck their heads. He could hear the hired hands banging off from the upstairs rooms. Soon, smoke was billowing in through the open windows, thickening the air. And now Rice grimly concluded that Corby had them at his mercy; he could storm in any time he wanted, or alternatively cook them alive if he torched the place like he had the bunkhouse.

Brad Silvers was peering through the open window, trying to glimpse some sign of movement out there against the leaping background of flame. Suddenly a gun cracked from closer at hand than he'd reckoned. The foreman jerked back, spun around, then sank to the floor. He sat holding his shoulder, blood seeping through his fingers. 'Ain't nothin' but a nick!' he grunted.

Lo Sang dragged the cloth from the table and ripped it to form a bandage. He crawled across to Silvers, bound it over his shirt to staunch the bleeding.

Rice wondered how the hired hands upstairs were faring. Silver's wound had somehow hammered home the desperate state they were in. Most likely none of them would get out of this alive — and the unfairness of it sickened him. Those boys defending the house from the first floor were defending a cause they had no knowledge of. Brad Silvers and Lo Sang would sacrifice their lives out of sheer cussedness, blind loyalty to two bosses who were already dead. Two other loyal Double Star cowboys had died when the herd had been stampeded and hundreds of beasts had perished. All were victims of one man's depraved lust for vengeance.

Now, Rice made up his mind quite suddenly. The only hope lay in striking at Vince Corby himself.

'I'm goin' out there,' he grunted. 'I'm goin' out to get Corby. It's the only way!'

Silvers eyed him as if he'd relinquished his sanity. 'They'll gun you down as soon as you step outside.'

'Maybe not if I go out the back. Maybe the back of the house isn't so well guarded.'

'You're crazy!' Silvers exclaimed.

'Maybe I am, but I'm sick of waitin' here like a sittin' duck. Blaze away through these windows, cause some sort of diversion.'

At last Silvers gave a reluctant nod. 'I'll let the boys know what's happenin'.'

Rice slipped cartridges into his six-shooter, grabbed his Winchester, then he moved across to the room where Able had fixed his bed. He stepped past the shrouded body to the window, gazed out. Everything seemed still, the bulk of the house shadowing the flames at the front. His best chance would be to get into the timber at the rear where it fringed Plum Creek. He should be able to angle round and reach the pasture fencing, then make a run towards the hay-barn which was currently ablaze. From there he must hope, pray, he could somehow get close enough to Corby to powder-burn him and make no mistake.

He eased back the clasp of the window, then struggled with the ancient sash to create an opening sufficient for him to squeeze through. At last he managed to slip his leg over the sill. Seconds later he was on the outside porch, crouching down against the wall, taking stock. Gunfire had taken on a new intensity at the front. Silvers and Lo Sang and the boys upstairs were blasting away, though he suspected that their bullets were not finding targets. Even so, he hoped that the outlaws would be keeping their heads down.

Taking a deep breath he launched himself forward, leaping over the porch railings. He hit the ground running, his injured leg long forgotten. He reached the trees unscathed and dropped down, gazing out for sight of his enemies. He could hear shouting. He wondered if Corby was preparing to play his final hand — by setting fire to the main house. A sense of urgency swept over him, hatred and fury boiling inside him. He had to find Corby if the men inside the house were to stand any chance of getting out alive.

So far he seemed to have gone unseen, but he had to circle around, get to the front of the main building. He came to his feet, ran further back into the timber, then followed the creek along until he emerged near the far fencing. He writhed beneath the bottom rail. Smoke was thickening all around; he could see the windmill, flames leaping up about its sails. Men were moving through the barns and outhouses, some hurling flaming torches upwards.

And right then he blundered into the hollow where the gang had left their horses. The wrangler guarding them leaped up. 'Hold on, mister . . . who the hell . . . ?' Rice caught him a crunching blow across the face with the butt of his Winchester, hurling him aside. For a second he ran between rearing horses, their ears back, their eyes rolling, their terrified whinnying fuelling the confusion. He rushed past the blazing bunkhouse and the windmill, around which flames licked like a devil's beacon — and ahead of him the ground fronting the ranch-house was bathed in fire-glow. He could hear men's voices coming from scattered points, and the fear was in him that he would never locate the one man he sought.

Rice paused, panting, drawing the hot, smoky air into his lungs, desperation akin to panic rising in him, the hopelessness of the situation merging into reality. Corby could be anywhere.

And then, as if fate was asserting its

contrary nature, Rice was startled by the shout — the familiar, deep voice he hated, hurling words out from the shadows of the nearby foaling sheds, and as his attention was drawn, he saw the outline of the man astride his big bay horse, shifting from the blackness into the flame-lit open, hands raised to his mouth as he sent that final, damning order to his men: '*OK, boys, the house is all yours. Burn it to a damned cinder!*'

Rice lifted the Winchester into his shoulder, took aim — yet instinct made him hold back. He knew he had come to kill this man, not match draws. He didn't *have* to see Corby's face or feel the burn of his eyes as he faced the eternity of coming death. He didn't *have* to make him realize that he was paying the penalty for all his sins and that it was Rice Sheridan who was administering that justice.

Even so he called out his name.

The big outlaw turned in his saddle, afforded Rice a sobering glimpse of the hard face with its beak-like nose, the murderous, crazed light in the deep-set eyes, the cruel twist of the mouth as he gasped, 'Kid!' . . . and then Rice pressed the trigger and the twin barrels of the Winchester roared.

Corby dissolved before his eyes. One moment he was sitting his saddle, solid as always — the next, there was only a vacuum and a suddenly rearing animal, its panicking hooves cleaving the air.

But Corby had not been alone. His men were moving from the shadows, their shouted surprise suddenly quelling the roar of gunfire. 'Vince's been shot!'

Rice's action had been observed. He could see men turning, yelling, pointing at him, raising their guns. Then those guns were belching flame and he felt the burn of passing lead. Completely vulnerable, he took the one avenue of escape that came to him. Leaping forward, almost into the guns of the men now coming for him, he found cover behind Corby's rearing bay. It was wild with fear.

Rice made a grab for the stirrup, then got his hand around the saddle horn. Somehow he hauled himself astride the animal, bracing himself to fight it, slamming with his heels to send it charging forward. Lethal lead was buzzing about his ears but he was beyond caring.

He galloped between blazing sheds and stables, cursing that such wickedness could be afflicted in the name of vengeance, not glancing back. Then he saw that his way was barred by a fence bordering a meadow. The bay showed no hesitation, carried him over it in an almighty leap and then repeated the feat on the far side — and now he was away. Only after a minute's hard gallop did he rein in and gaze back upon the turmoil. Thankfully the house hadn't yet been put to the torch; he hoped the shooting of Vince Corby had shocked his men into holding back.

He wondered if Corby had been killed or merely wounded. He circled on to higher ground, aware that most of

219

the gunfire from below had faded out.

He debated what his best course of action now was. Should he leave the wounded Brad Silvers and the others to whatever fate felt prudent to inflict, should he ride for Bull Crossing to discover whether or not Harry Allchurch had summoned the Texas Rangers? But he knew that would take hours, that all might be lost by the time help arrived. For a long while he sat there, holding in Corby's mighty horse, feeling strangely detached from all that had happened. Uncertainty drove him to favour one course of action, then the other. Eventually, as he saw the first glimmer of dawn on the far rims and the shadows receding from the hollows, he made up his mind. He would ride back to the ranch. But even as he touched his heels to the big bay, he heard the pound of approaching horses and, gazing out towards Travis Mountain, saw riders streaming towards the ranch. He strained his eyes through the early, smoke-hazed light until he was sure his vision was not playing a cruel trick. Only then did relief cut through him. Matters had been taken out of his hands. A company of Texas Rangers had arrived — not summoned by Marshal Harry Allchurch, as Rice now supposed, but by the Pinkerton man Schwartz.

Within the next twenty minutes, Corby's marauders had vanished into the half-light of dawn, leaving three dead, the fight gone out of them, the havoc left at the Double Star a grim reminder of one man's evil quest for vengeance.

Rice Sheridan rode down to the ranch, spoke briefly with the group of heavily armed Rangers who were gazing at the brain-shot body of the outlaw leader. Afterwards, he entered the house and found a grateful Brad Silvers, Lo Sang and three ranch-hands — shocked, dazed and scarcely able to believe that the danger had passed.

21

Rice kept the big bay horse, feeling that was the least Corby owed him. Next day, when he returned to Bull Crossing, he learned about the strange death of Harry Allchurch at the hands of the Pinkerton man — and he had no idea what had brought about the tragedy.

When Rice unsaddled Corby's horse and searched through the saddle-bags, he found an assortment of baggage that was inevitable for a man who ran beyond the law, who lived by the bullet — ammunition, an extra Colt .45, a sharp-honed bowie knife, a collection of Wanted-notices, showing his own face — but there were two items that were surprising. Firstly, there was an old Bible and, as Rice thumbed through the tattered pages, he discovered a passage in Proverbs underlined. *Whoso causeth the righteous to go astray in an evil way, he shall fall himself into his own pit.* He read the words aloud, found their sentiment chilling.

He also found an old photograph, its sepia creased, soiled and faded but its image was clear even so . . . a photograph of a youthful Vince Corby, his eyes not deep-sunken, his face not soured, as Rice remembered, by bitterness — and with him was a young woman, seated and gazing with loving and proud eyes at the baby in her arms. Seeing the small family group brought a lump to Rice's throat. Here was a side to the man he had not considered — a side that portrayed Corby as a human being and not as a monster intent only on murder and revenge.

In the days that followed, Rice spent all the time he could with Maggie, finding her companionship soothing and wonderful, and his love for her grew ever stronger. He worked with Brad Silvers, now recovering from his bullet wound. They restored the ranch to the best of their ability as they awaited future events to unfold. By the late summer, sufficient beasts had been rounded up to justify herding them to market up the Chisholm Trail. Fresh cow-hands were taken on to accomplish this. Rice did not go with them, there was still much work to be done at the ranch — and also, he had no desire to leave Maggie.

In October, he received an official looking letter from William Tuttle, attorney at law in San Antonio, requesting that he visit his offices. Maggie accompanied him when he made the journey by stage, helped him find the legal practice near to the impressive Casino Theatre, and was presently sitting alongside him as Tuttle, a frosty-looking man with spiky sideburns, explained the contents of Able Early's will, delivered to San Antonio by Carl Schwartz.

The declaration therein altered Rice's life forever — not so much by the fact that, as an effort to salve his troubled conscience, Able had left to Rice the Double Star and the remaining Early wealth, which despite the loss of the prime-beef herd and certain gambling losses, was still substantial — but by the testament, written in faltering hand, that was attached. Rice and Maggie listened attentively as the lawyer cleared his throat and read aloud the words Able had penned shortly before his death.

'The truth cannot rest dormant inside me any longer. I know what we did at the Sheridan homestead was wicked beyond forgiveness, and it must now be made clear that it was not the Indians who carried out the massacre, but my brother Seth, Harry Allchurch and myself — and we must all bear the responsibility for the sins that were committed that day.'

'What are you sayin'?' Rice exclaimed, rising from his chair.

'What I read is self-explanatory, Mister Sheridan. Whatever preconceived notions you had about your past must now be revised. I suggest you listen calmly while I read the rest of this document.'

Rice attempted to speak, but all he managed was an indignant gasp. Gently, Maggie pulled him down onto his chair.

'The liquor turned us into crazed and lustful brutes,' Tuttle continued. 'None of us intended Laurina Sheridan should die at our hands. But it happened, and nothing can alter events . . . '

'Oh God!' Again Rice interrupted, his face working with emotion, but the lawyer pressed on.

'When we set the soddy ablaze, our hope was that all evidence would be destroyed, that everything would be forgotten and nobody would suspect the truth. In due course folks accepted that the Indians were guilty and never an accusing finger was pointed at us . . . but that didn't stop the guilt festering inside us. And when we first saw the man who called himself Vince Corby we knew that his true identity was Grant Sheridan whom we had shot and left for dead at the soddy. Only then, with horror, did we realize that he had somehow survived the wound, perhaps saved from the flames by the sudden downpour of rain — and that he had escaped, hiding his identity with a false name, forever swearing vengeance for what had happened to his woman and homestead . . . '

Rice was on his feet again, Maggie's restraining hand gripping his arm. His face was pale. 'I can't believe it,' he gasped. 'I can't believe it!'

The lawyer had paused, gazing with exasperation over the top of his spectacles. 'There is no doubt about it, Mister Sheridan. The truth is here for all to see.'

'D'you realize what you're tellin' me?' Rice demanded. He swallowed hard. 'You're tellin' me I killed my own father?'

'I cannot change, nor condone, what has happened, Mister Sheridan. I can only convey the facts.'

Maggie had taken the photograph of Corby and his young family from her bag, her hazel eyes wide with astonishment. 'So this baby is you, Rice. It's incredible!'

But despite her astonishment, Maggie absorbed the knowledge more readily than Rice himself. He was to spend long moments staring at the photograph, even touching, with respectful fingers, the faces of his mother and father — until eventually he came to accept the truth; accept the fact that the Earlys, whom he'd respected and served, were responsible for his own traumatic childhood — and for sowing the bitter seed of vengeance into the heart of the man they had so dreadfully wronged.

But the most grievous scar that Rice Sheridan suffered was the knowledge that he had killed his own father. Gazing again and again at the photograph, he saw the youthful hope that shone from the eyes of his parents, hope that was smashed by Seth and

Able Early and Harry Allchurch.

Rice wept at the knowledge, wondering if his father had ever suspected who he was but hoping he had not. His chagrin was somehow shared by Maggie, and she consoled him and expressed no doubt that what he had done was right. 'You had no option,' she told him. 'Vince Corby couldn't be allowed to live. It was your duty to destroy the evil that had grown up. It must have been God's will, Rice.'

'God's will!' He reached out, held her hand, striving desperately to share her reasoning. It was hard to accept, but he tried, and from that time on, all youthful recklessness drained out of him. He viewed his inheritance as distasteful. Anything that was tainted by the Earlys was repulsive to him. 'I don't want the ranch, Magdalen,' he told her. 'I could never live there. It'd be too full of memories.'

She made no comment, but he felt the warmth of her understanding.

And then in a humble voice he

asked, 'What should I do, Magdalen?'

She thought for a moment, then said, 'You should sell the ranch. Take the money and build a new life.'

Rice looked at her, drawing strength from her pragmatism, from her wisdom, seeing in her sweet face his own future. He needed her strength now, just as he would need it for the rest of his life.

In the following weeks, the Double Star was put up for sale and in the spring a good offer was received. There was also a reward paid by the state for the capture, dead or alive, of Vince Corby, but Rice handed this money over to the town committee who used it to finance the first church in that community. Seamus Finnegan took retirement, sold his practice and lived locally, patronizing the saloon and delivering an occasional baby. He found joy in the knowledge that the girl he loved as a daughter, and who forever kept a caring and sometimes reproving eye on him, found fruitful fulfilment with the young man of her choice. After their marriage, Rice built a cabin on the outskirts of town and subsequently became marshal of Bull Crossing. He served in that capacity for some thirty years.

In the town's cemetery he erected a stone over Vince Corby's previously unmarked grave. Beneath the outlaw's true name he had the following words inscribed. *He Died Administering the Word of the Bible. Whoso causeth the righteous to go astray in an evil way, he shall fall himself into his own pit.*

Other titles in the
Linford Western Library

THE CROOKED SHERIFF
John Dyson

Black Pete Bowen quit Texas with a burning hatred of men who try to take the law into their own hands. But he discovers that things aren't much different in the silver mountains of Arizona.

THEY'LL HANG BILLY
FOR SURE:
Larry & Stretch
Marshall Grover

Billy Reese, the West's most notorious desperado, was to stand trial. From all compass points came the curious and the greedy, the riff-raff of the frontier. Suddenly, a crazed killer was on the loose — but the Texas Trouble-Shooters were there, girding their loins for action.